"I wanted to check on Rhett."

He moved closer, crowding her a little. But she didn't step back. She stood her ground. "That's not all you want," he whispered.

There weren't enough words in the English language to cover all the things she wanted from David. From life. From this moment.

"Ask me again," he told her, threading his fingers through her hair. The desire she saw in his blue eyes mesmerized her. A longing that matched her own, making her need grow that much more intense. "Ask me to have an affair with you."

"Kiss me," she said instead. Those two words were the only ones she could force her mouth to form at the moment.

He lowered his mouth to hers, claiming her lips with a force she felt all the way to her toes. How could the way he touched her feel both infinitely gentle and demanding at the same time? She wound her arms around his neck and gave herself over to the sensation. It was too much and not enough, and she whispered the one word that pounded through her whole body, "More."

* * *

CRIMSON, COLORADO:
Finding home—and forever—in the West

Dear Reader,

I feel so fortunate that my kids had so many amazing teachers as they went through elementary school. A great teacher who connects with students can make such a difference in a child's life, so it was an honor to base the character of Erin MacDonald on two of my favorite real-life teachers here in Colorado. As a heroine, Erin has a huge heart and a deep commitment to her students in Crimson, although she's used to living life on the sidelines, so she doesn't quite recognize everything she has to offer.

But she can't help but get involved with David McCay and his young nephew, Rhett. Both of them touch her heart, and she's willing to come out of her shell to make sure they find the healing they need. For his part, David isn't used to taking help from anyone, especially not a sweet, soft-spoken kindergarten teacher. But Erin is exactly what he needs to help him leave behind his complicated history and claim the life and love he truly wants.

I hope you enjoy reading their story as much as I loved writing it. I love to hear from readers. You can find me on Facebook, Twitter or at www.michellemajor.com.

Big hugs,

Michelle

Romancing the Wallflower

Michelle Major

HARLEQUIN® SPECIAL EDITION®

ISBN-13: 978-0-373-62369-3

Romancing the Wallflower

This edition published by arrangement with Harlequin Books S.A.

For questions and comments about the quality of this book, please contact us at CustomerService@Harlequin.com.

Printed in U.S.A.

Michelle Major grew up in Ohio but dreamed of living in the mountains. Soon after graduating with a degree in journalism, she pointed her car west and settled in Colorado. Her life and house are filled with one great husband, two beautiful kids, a few furry pets and several well-behaved reptiles. She's grateful to have found her passion writing stories with happy endings. Michelle loves to hear from her readers at michellemajor.com.

Books by Michelle Major

Harlequin Special Edition

Crimson, Colorado

Christmas on Crimson Mountain
Always the Best Man
A Baby and a Betrothal
A Very Crimson Christmas
Suddenly a Father
A Second Chance on Crimson Ranch
A Kiss on Crimson Ranch

A Brevia Beginning
Her Accidental Engagement
Still the One

The Fortunes of Texas: The Secret Fortune

A Fortune in Waiting

The Fortunes of Texas: All Fortune's Children

Fortune's Special Delivery

The Fortunes of Texas: Cowboy Country

The Taming of Delaney Fortune

Visit the Author Profile page
at Harlequin.com for more titles.

To all my favorite Broadmoor Elementary teachers.
Thanks for everything you do for our kids.

Chapter One

"Stop staring at the hottie brewmaster's butt."

Erin MacDonald choked on the gulp of strawberry daiquiri she'd just swallowed. "I'm not staring at anyone's butt," she said as she grabbed a wad of napkins and dabbed at her chin and shirtfront. "And don't talk so loud."

Melody Cross, one of the second-grade teachers at Crimson Elementary, snorted. "It's a crowded bar on a busy Thursday night. No one can hear me."

But Melody had the kind of booming voice that could quiet a room full of squirming eight-year-olds the afternoon before summer break. The tall table they stood at was a good five feet from the bar, but Erin swore she saw the man's broad shoulders stiffen.

"Want me to take a picture of him?" Suzie Vitale, her fellow kindergarten teacher, offered with a tipsy smile. "It lasts longer."

Before Erin could stop her, the curvy blonde aimed her

phone at the backside of the gorgeous guy who not only worked the bar but also owned Elevation Brewery. The brewpub had opened a little over a year ago and had become a popular hangout for both locals and tourists in the quaint mountain town of Crimson, Colorado.

Erin had noticed David McCay, the brewery's owner, the first time she'd stepped into the nouveau rustic—and very on-trend for Colorado—space. He was tall and lean, with dark blond hair that curled around the collars of the flannel shirts he favored. David McCay was as handsome as a movie star and built like he spent endless hours tossing huge sacks of barley—or whatever it was beer brewers did.

Erin, who was built like she spent her days sitting cross-legged on a reading rug, had surreptitiously watched him each time she came into the bar with friends or coworkers for a random happy hour or birthday celebration. He was often tending bar or sometimes she'd spot him coming out from the back, wearing the heavy rubber boots and backward ball cap that she'd quickly learned were his uniform when actually brewing beer.

Colorado was known for its craft brews, and the fact that Elevation had made a name for itself so quickly was a testament to his hard work and talent at running a business.

At least that's what Erin wanted to believe. Her mother liked to remind Erin that she too often assumed the best about people, which allowed them to regularly take advantage of her.

But David McCay hadn't taken advantage of her, even though it was the stuff of her fantasies. Even though his nephew, Rhett, was now in her kindergarten class and David had been with the boy and his mother for back-to-school night. Erin had barely been able to put a sentence together with David towering over the other adults in the back of her classroom, but he hadn't bothered to acknowledge her. Heck, it was doubtful he even knew she existed.

Except when she blinked and looked up, he was staring straight at her. Sparks of awareness flamed through her body, setting every inch of her skin on fire. He lifted one thick brow as if he could read her thoughts. Which might be impossible since it felt like all of her brain cells had spontaneously combusted under the weight of his stare.

She heard Melody giggle behind her, and Suzie gave her a little shove forward. David now stood at the edge of the bar, only a short distance from her, with movement all around him. Customers in groups laughed and talked. A waitress set her tray on the rich wood bar top. A group of women near the edge of the bar vied for his attention. But his focus remained on Erin.

Then something—someone—suddenly blocked her vision. Cole Bennett, Crimson's recently elected sheriff, was talking to David. Cole was also tall and broad, and to use one of her mom's favorite expressions, made a better door than a window.

Erin shifted to the right as she overheard Cole mention Rhett, David's nephew. David's gaze hardened and his jaw clenched. Unable to stop herself, she moved forward, sidestepping a couple heading toward the back of the bar and a group of twentysomething guys who looked like they'd just come off a hiking trail, until she stood directly behind the sheriff.

She was five feet four inches tall in the clogs she favored for work, so both men towered over her and were completely unaware she was listening to their conversation. Invisibility was Erin's unintentional superpower. She knew much more than she should about her coworkers and neighbors, simply because people didn't notice she was there.

"Rhett is safe," Cole told David. "But they can't get him to come out."

"What the hell was Jenna thinking?" David asked, then scrubbed a hand over his jaw. "No, don't answer that."

"She's in trouble, David. The crowd she's running with—"

"I'll handle it." He pulled a set of keys out of one of the pockets in his tan cargo pants. "I just need to tell Tracie I'm leaving for the night. I'll be over for Rhett."

"I have to call Social Services," Cole said softly, and Erin felt the tension ratchet up a notch.

"Give me some time with him first, okay?"

"Can you—"

"I'll handle it," David repeated. He moved behind the bar and spoke to the woman filling two pint glasses from the tap.

The sheriff walked out of the bar, patrons instinctively clearing a path for him although he wasn't in uniform tonight.

When she looked up, David McCay stood toe-to-toe with her. She realized she'd moved forward to block his path from behind the bar.

In her daydreams, she'd compared his eyes to the brilliant summer sky above the ragged peak of Crimson Mountain or the iridescent cobalt of a tropical lagoon. But now his frosty stare was more like the ice blue of a glacier, so cold a shiver passed through her.

"I don't have time for this, sweetheart. You and your friends are going to have to play your liquid courage bar games with someone else."

"It's not a game," Erin said.

"Darlin', you ordered a froofy drink in my bar. It's either a game or a joke."

This close to David, the heat and frustration radiating off him made her feel different from the woman she knew herself to be. She was aware of her body in a way that was new and exhilarating. She wanted more. She wanted… something she couldn't name. Still, the promise of it made her weak with longing.

Also braver than she'd ever been. Or maybe *crazy* was a better word, because when he moved to step around her, she placed a hand on his arm.

"I can help with your nephew."

His sleeves were rolled up to the elbow. His skin burned hers, and the rough hair on his forearm tickled her fingers. A current passed through him, the force jolting Erin like she'd been struck by lightning. He stilled and the power it took to rein in all the things she imagined he was feeling right now made an answering strength bubble up inside her.

"Let me help, David." It was the first time she'd spoken his name out loud. To her friends, he was simply "the hottie brewmaster."

"You're drunk," he said, his gaze focused on where her fingers wrapped around his arm.

"No. I only had one drink. I'm fine now. Promise." She lifted her hand. "Rhett is in my class," she said, in case this enormous, angry man truly had no idea who she was.

"I know." One side of his mouth almost quirked. "I came to back-to-school night."

So she wasn't quite invisible to David McCay. A little thrill tickled down her spine. "I've connected with him. He responds to me."

David's cool blue gaze met hers again, and he gave a brief nod. "Let's go then."

Erin swallowed. This was really happening. "I just need to tell my friends I'm leaving."

"My truck is out front," he said, his voice a low rumble. Then he turned and walked away. Erin had the distinct impression if she didn't get her butt in gear, he'd readily leave her behind.

No chance she was letting that happen.

"I've got to go," she said as she rushed to where Melody and Suzie stood gawking. She grabbed her purse from the tabletop.

"With the hottie brewmaster?" Melody asked, her voice a high squeak.

Suzie pumped a fist. "No beating around the bush tonight."

"It's not like that." Erin glanced over her shoulder but David was already out the door. "I can't explain now. I'll see you at school tomorrow."

Before her friends could respond, she hurried toward the brewpub's entrance. The young, flawlessly mountain-chic brunette at the hostess stand gave her the once-over and arched a brow, wordlessly communicating that a woman like Erin had no business following David McCay out into the night.

Normally Erin would agree, but this was more than her hidden crush on the man. It was about helping a troubled five-year-old boy. Erin's students were family to her, and she took her responsibility to heart. She had a Spidey sense for the ones who needed a little extra; whether it was the child or their family circumstances, Erin made it her mission to connect with every student in her care.

From the moment Rhett McCay had slunk into her classroom clutching his beautiful mother's arm, Erin's radar had been on high alert. Jenna McCay clearly loved her son, yet the woman seemed high-strung and flighty.

Erin had the impression Rhett's home life was anything but stable.

She might not have the guts to talk to David on her own, but she was fearless when it came to one of her kids.

A huge black Chevy truck idled near the curb, and she knew David was behind the wheel. Not that she was a stalker or anything, but Crimson was a small town and she'd seen him drop off and pick up Rhett at school several times.

"I'm fearless," she whispered to herself when her legs wanted to stop on the sidewalk. It was late September and the evening air was crisp, the changing season scenting the breeze.

If Erin were an ice cream flavor, she would be straight-up vanilla. Everything about her life was ordinary, ordered and infinitely normal. Somehow she knew getting into David's truck was going to add a whole slew of strange toppings to the mix. She might long for adventure, but this wasn't what she had in mind.

She conjured up Rhett's sweet face, with his shaggy blond bowl cut and mischievous blue eyes. With a calming breath she moved forward, opened the passenger-side door and climbed in.

"You ready?" David asked in that deep, hot-caramel-syrup voice of his.

Absolutely not, Erin thought.

"I'm ready," she answered.

David was going to kill his little sister, if she didn't manage the task on her own first.

He concentrated on navigating the route from the bar to Jenna's small apartment complex on the outskirts of Crimson as fast as he could without breaking any laws. He took slow breaths in and out to calm himself. Of course any thoughts of doing her harm were a joke, although she seemed hell-bent on getting into as much trouble as she could find.

Which had been one thing when they were teenagers, but Jenna had Rhett now. The constant stream of dead-end jobs, loser boyfriends and wild partying wasn't only hurting her. The thought that Rhett would end up somehow irreparably scarred kept David up more nights than he cared to admit.

He'd moved to Crimson from Pittsburgh almost two years ago to watch out for them. But between the hours he'd put in opening the brewery and Jenna's resentment over what she saw as his attempts to control her life, he hadn't spent nearly as much time with them as he wanted.

His greatest fear was that he would fail his nephew the same way he'd failed Jenna.

"I'm guessing you and your sister are pretty close?"

David blinked and glanced at the woman sitting next to him in the truck's cab. Lost in his own thoughts, he'd almost forgotten about his uninvited passenger. What the hell had possessed him to allow Rhett's kindergarten teacher to come along on this mission anyway?

David was a master at keeping everyone in his life at arm's length, even Jenna and Rhett. How had this tiny woman with the thick ponytail the color of maple syrup and big eyes to match managed to slip through his defenses?

"We're Irish twins," he offered as an answer. "Ten months apart."

"That must have been fun growing up," she said, her voice gentle. The exact kind of voice that could lull a classroom of restless kids into sitting in a quiet circle to learn. Most kids anyway. He still had trouble believing Rhett could calm his squirmy body enough to sit still.

"Not for our mom."

She gave a small laugh. "If Rhett takes after the two of you, your mother had her hands full."

"Yeah," he agreed, and felt the knot in his chest loosen slightly at the affection in her voice. David had no problem with his nephew's rambunctious personality, but he was normally in the minority.

He didn't say anything more, and Erin didn't speak for a few minutes. David liked quiet, but other than Tracie at the bar, most women he knew couldn't tolerate it. The silence that filled his truck now was strangely comforting, like an extra blanket thrown over the bed on a cold winter night. Like all good things, it didn't last.

"What happened tonight? Is your sister in trouble? Is Rhett okay?"

David sighed. He knew the questions were coming, and he owed the soft-spoken teacher an explanation before they reached the apartment. "How much did you overhear from Cole?"

"No details. Just that there was a problem and Rhett wasn't cooperating."

"He's hiding," he said, trying in vain to stop the anger and frustration from trickling into his voice. He could feel it seeping through his pores, making his blood run hot and raging. "Apparently he's wedged under the kitchen sink. Jenna had a party, and things got out of hand. The cops busted it up and found drugs."

Erin gave a sharp intake of breath, rousing his temper even further, like a backdraft making a fire blaze out of control. "Jenna loves that boy with all her heart, but she's in a bad way. It's why I moved to Crimson in the first place."

"To help your sister?"

To save her, he wanted to answer, but he only nodded.

David knew his limitations better than anyone, and he was nobody's hero.

"She's been clean for almost two years," he said without emotion. "It's been tough, but I thought she had her demons under control. Cole took everyone to the station. They didn't realize Rhett was there until the place was empty and he made a noise. The deputies tried to get him out, but he freaked and scratched one of the officers. I know Cole so he called me before the social worker."

He bit the inside of his cheek and waited for the recrimination he deserved. He should have seen the signs that Jenna was teetering on the edge. He knew her better than anyone. Why the hell couldn't he keep her safe?

He pulled into the parking lot of the shabby apartment complex. There were two buildings, both with faded siding and balconies that looked like they wouldn't hold the weight of a litter of kittens. He'd begged Jenna to let him help her move to a better place, but his sister was stubborn and resented any time he tried to "take control" of her life.

"We'll make sure he's safe," Erin said as he turned off the truck's engine.

Safe. The word had haunted him—and tainted every relationship in his life—for over a decade. Now this too-sweet-for-her-own-good woman offered it to his nephew like she had that kind of power. Damn if David didn't want to believe it was true.

He shifted to face her, the dim light of the parking lot illuminating her face so that her creamy skin looked like something out of a dream. Unable to resist, he ran the pad of his thumb over the ridge of her cheekbone, marveling at how soft her skin felt.

The inherent goodness radiating from her drew him in at the same time he knew he should push her away. Someone like Erin MacDonald had no business knowing the ugly details of his sister's struggles. She was Rhett's teacher and nothing more. But he couldn't let her go quite yet. Tonight she was his talisman. He had to believe having her close would keep the darkness always skirting the edges of his life at bay.

He dropped his hand and they got out of the truck and started toward Jenna's apartment. Toward the little boy David was determined to keep safe, by any means necessary.

Chapter Two

"Come on, buddy. You've got to come out."

The muscles bunched in David's broad shoulders as he shifted his weight to one arm and leaned closer, reaching into the open cabinet under the kitchen sink.

A high-pitched scream split the air and several bottles of household cleaners tumbled out onto the scuffed linoleum floor.

David sat back on his knees with a muttered curse. "He bit me," he said, examining the back of his hand where a semicircle of angry red teeth marks was clearly visible.

"Same thing happened to me," Cole Bennett whispered. Cole had been waiting at Jenna McCay's cramped apartment, clearing out the other officers when David and Erin arrived. "I didn't want to force him out because I was worried he'd get hurt banging his head on the pipes if he struggled."

The two men, both so strong, looked absolutely baffled

at how to lure the young boy from his hiding spot. Erin glanced around the apartment and suppressed a shudder. On every surface, abandoned beer bottles and red plastic cups competed for space with fast-food wrappers and empty chip bags. It looked like a college fraternity house the morning after a huge party. The colorful drawings stuck to the front of the refrigerator were the only hint that a kindergartner lived here.

One of the crayoned pieces of art gave Erin an idea. She moved toward the narrow hallway, stepping over trash until she got to a half-open bedroom door. The space was neat and clean, untouched by the mess in the rest of the apartment. Toys lined one wall and the small bed was covered with a football-themed comforter. She grabbed the stuffed blue dog sitting on top of the pillow and hurried back to the kitchen.

David was once again on all fours in front of the cabinet, speaking so softly she couldn't make out his words, only the rough yet surprisingly gentle timbre of his voice.

She crouched low next to him and tilted her head until she could see Rhett's eyes, wide and still terrified. "Rhett," she said, "It's Ms. MacDonald. I found your stuffed dog and wanted to let you know he's okay."

A faint whimper came from the cabinet. "Ruffie," the boy whispered.

"Ruffie is safe," Erin said, using the same tone she would when soothing a child scared of letting go of his mother's leg on the first day of school. "You're safe, too. Your uncle David is going to take care of you. But we need you to come out now."

The boy wedged himself farther into the corner, as if he could make himself invisible. God, Erin did *not* want this child to feel like he needed to be invisible. David's large hand settled on the small of her back, and the steady pressure and warmth of his skin were more of a comfort than she would have guessed.

"Ruffie needs you." She placed the small dog in front of her, just on the edge of the cabinet. "He's scared and needs a hug. Can you do that for him?"

She held her breath for what felt like an eternity, then released it as the boy slowly unfolded his body and climbed out. Her fingers remained wrapped around the stuffed animal's back leg to make sure Rhett wouldn't try to grab it and retreat again.

Once he was in the light, she could see the smudge of dirt on his chin and the tearstains on his ruddy cheeks. Her heart broke for what this young boy had already seen in his life. David made a sound low in his throat and scooped up his nephew and the raggedy blue dog. It was as if a dam broke in Rhett and his whole body began to shake as he burrowed into David's embrace.

She straightened and stepped away, closer to the sheriff. Somehow it felt wrong to bear witness to the moment between David and Rhett, both tender and raw. It was obvious David was trying to keep his emotions hidden, but pain and guilt were bright on his handsome features, like a stoplight in the dark.

"Nice work," Cole Bennett said and put a hand on her elbow to lead her to the apartment door. "You're like a kindergartner whisperer." She started to turn but stopped at the sound of David's voice.

"Stay."

One word, but the intensity of it rocked her to her core.

She glanced up at Cole, who arched a brow.

"I'll stay," she told him.

He nodded. "Someone from Social Services will be here soon. I can let them in. They'll want to talk to David and the boy."

"We'll be ready," she said with more confidence than she felt.

She turned back and followed David to the couch, quickly cleaning off the coffee table and dumping everything into the trash before lowering herself next to him.

Rhett still clung to him, chubby fingers holding fistfuls of flannel shirt in a death grip. "Where's Mommy?" he asked in a tiny voice.

"She's…" David paused and his gaze slammed into hers. The pain in his eyes made her want to wrap her arms around both him and Rhett and make this whole night go away. "She's safe. Sheriff Bennett is taking care of her."

Erin wondered exactly how Jenna McCay was being cared for, and she hoped that whatever was happening Jenna was coherent enough to feel horrible about the situation she'd created for her son.

"It was loud," Rhett said. "Mommy's friends woke me up. I came out to tell her, but there were so many grown-ups and I couldn't find her. Then everyone started yelling and I got scared and hid under the sink."

"That was real smart of you," David told the boy, his hand smoothing Rhett's sleep-tousled hair.

After a moment Rhett tipped up his head to look at David. "When is Mommy coming home?"

"I'm not sure, buddy. But I'll stay with you until she does, okay?"

Rhett chewed on his bottom lip for a few seconds, then nodded. After a knock at the door, Cole let in a gray-haired woman who appeared to be in her midfifties. She wore a plain white button-down shirt and dark pants and looked about as no-nonsense as they came.

The woman spoke to Cole in hushed tones for a few minutes, then they both approached.

"This is Becky Cramer from the county Human Services department," Cole said.

Becky gave David a small nod, then bent to look at Rhett. "You've had quite a night," she said gently.

"It was loud," Rhett said, turning in David's lap but not releasing his shirtfront.

"I'm David McCay." David offered the woman his hand. "Rhett's uncle. He'll stay with me while we sort out things with Jenna."

Becky shook his hand, then glanced at Erin.

"I'm Rhett's kindergarten teacher, Erin MacDonald." She saw a flash of surprise pass over Becky's sharp features.

Right. How was she supposed to explain why she'd ended up on the couch with David and Rhett, caught up in the middle of family drama that had started long past regular school hours?

"Erin is a friend of mine," David answered. Becky seemed to have no issue with that response, whereas Erin had trouble keeping her jaw from hitting the floor. Friends with David McCay? In what lifetime?

Men like David didn't have boring kindergarten teachers as friends. Before he came to Crimson, he'd been a major-league baseball pitcher. He must be used to drop-dead gorgeous women who were exciting and sexy.

Erin knew she was boring. And ordinary. Not at all David's type. She'd had a boyfriend last year—an accountant at a firm in town. He was quiet, average and exactly her type. Greg had broken up with her to date someone who was better than average, but that didn't mean Erin could change the person she was on the inside. No matter how much she wanted to try.

David had been her unrequited crush since the moment she'd first seen him. It was a harmless fantasy with no chance of rejection. Never had she expected to get to know him, let alone be part of his life in this kind of personal way.

Her mind drifted to that moment in the car when he'd traced his thumb over her cheekbone. The simple touch had sent shock waves rippling through her and ignited a kind of flash-point desire Erin hadn't realized she was capable of feeling.

"It's important the school and the family work together," Becky said, bringing Erin back to the current conversation with a jolt, "to keep the boy's life as stable as possible during this time."

She looked at Rhett, who had fallen asleep in David's arms. "Let me put him to bed," she whispered, "while you two finish talking."

David relaxed his grip, allowing her to lift the boy into her arms. She made sure to take the stuffed dog, too. Rhett remained asleep as she tucked him back into bed, sighing when his head hit the pillow. Erin sat on the mattress for several minutes, rubbing the boy's back to make sure he didn't wake again. She couldn't imagine how scared he must have been earlier, unable to find his mother and with the wild party in full swing.

She made a silent vow. She *would* keep him safe, no matter how far out of her comfort zone—and tangled up with David McCay—that led her.

It was almost two in the morning before David let himself into the apartment, exhausted and emotionally drained. Erin had agreed to stay while he went to see Jenna. Cole was keeping her overnight on possession charges but had agreed to drop them if she entered a rehab program.

David had helped his sister get clean once before, and it

was a rough road. She swore that tonight's tumble off the wagon was a onetime occurrence. David wanted to believe her, yet he'd heard so many excuses over the years. All he knew was he had to protect his nephew. There could be no repeats of what Rhett had gone through tonight.

It never should have happened in the first place, and he couldn't stop blaming himself.

The apartment was quiet when he entered, and he found Erin asleep on the couch, curled on her side as if she didn't want to take up too much space. It blew his mind that the buttoned-up schoolteacher had so willingly pitched in to help with his hot mess of a life. He understood that Rhett was her student. But David had never encountered a teacher like her.

Hell, he would have paid a lot more attention in school if he'd had someone like Erin MacDonald in his corner.

If possible, she looked more luminously beautiful asleep than she did awake. She was like a damn fairy-tale princess with her creamy skin, straight nose, rosy cheeks and the long, dark hair that fell over her face. It was easier to study her now than when those too-knowing bourbon-colored eyes were staring back at him.

He covered her with a blanket and went to check on Rhett. Unlike Erin, the boy was sprawled across the bed, arms and legs reaching out like a starfish. Jenna claimed she'd meant to have only her new boyfriend and a few of his buddies to the house to watch the Broncos play, but things had gotten out of hand. According to Cole, the boy-friend was serious bad news, having had more than a few run-ins with law enforcement over the years.

How the hell did Jenna manage to attract the biggest scumbags on the planet every time she found a new man? He would have asked her, wanted to rail and shout, but she'd looked so defeated sitting alone in the holding cell.

She understood she'd messed up and he knew from experience that heaping on more condemnation would only put her on the defensive.

Fear and guilt had warred in his sister's pale blue eyes, along with the remnants of a long-ago pain that she could hide from most of the world, but not from him. She'd agreed to check into a treatment program, so finding a place for her would be the first thing on his to-do list after getting Rhett to school in a few hours.

He lowered himself into the recliner next to the couch. Erin had cleaned the messy apartment, another debt of thanks he owed her. David hated owing people anything, had learned the hard way to only depend on himself. Yet he couldn't help but be grateful for the chance to simply sit and rest for a few minutes.

His eyes drifted shut, although he didn't intend to fall asleep. The next thing he knew, someone was shaking him awake. He blinked and found himself staring into Erin's huge brown eyes.

"I have to go," she whispered. "I need to shower and change before school."

David blinked and tried to look more with-it than he felt. "What time is it?"

"Almost six in the morning." She moved away and he had the ridiculous urge to pull her down against him. These past few hours had been the soundest he'd slept in years. Something about having this woman close soothed the demons that waited for him in the dark.

"I'll give you a ride," he told her, rising from the chair. His lower back ached, and as he looked around the small apartment, reality came crashing over him like a tidal wave. Today was going to be awful. "I'll need to wake Rhett and—"

"One of my girlfriends is on her way." Erin shoved a

thick lock of hair behind one ear. "Rhett needs all the sleep he can get. He's coming to school today, right?"

"Yes," David answered, mentally listing all the things he had to get done. "He needs a routine now more than ever."

"How's your sister?"

"She feels terrible and says she's committed to straightening out her life once and for all. I need to pick her up this morning and then make arrangements to get her to a treatment facility."

"So Rhett will be staying with you while she's in rehab?"

"Yes. Not here. I live in a loft above the brewery."

"How long is the program?"

He sighed. "A month. Rhett doesn't know she'll be gone. I'll tell him when he wakes up, but she won't leave until tomorrow afternoon. I want him to spend time with her—to know that she's okay."

"It could be traumatic," Erin said with a nod. "But we'll get him through."

He didn't want to admit how much her words resonated with him. When had he suddenly become afraid of dealing with things on his own? David prided himself on never being dependent on anyone, let alone a woman who'd been a stranger only twelve hours ago.

She worried her bottom lip between her teeth, a nervous habit he'd seen her do several times since they'd left the bar. That moment when he'd caught her staring at his ass felt like a lifetime ago.

He ran a finger across the seam of her lips. "You need to give that lip a break. It's too pretty to take so much abuse."

"Oh," she breathed, pink rushing into her cheeks. He wasn't sure what had surprised her more—his touch or the fact that he thought her mouth was pretty. Pretty and far too kissable to be good for either of them.

"I appreciate your help," he said, the words rusty and unfamiliar on his tongue. "I'm going to make sure Rhett has a stable home life, but having a teacher who understands what he's going through will be important."

She inclined her head to study him. After everything she'd witnessed and what she'd clearly inferred about the dysfunctional McCay family, it must seem odd for him to suddenly be speaking so formally.

"Of course." Her brows knit together, causing a small crease to appear on her forehead. He resisted the urge to smooth it away…barely. "I should go. Melody doesn't live far from here. She'll be waiting."

She moved across the small space, and he didn't say anything until the door to the apartment had almost closed.

"Erin."

She turned, one hand on the doorknob. "Yes?"

"I'd like to repay you for last night." The thought of remaining in debt to her—to anyone—chafed his skin like an itch he couldn't quite reach.

"There's no need—"

"There *is* a need." The need pounding through him to claim her. He tried to convince himself the longing would be quenched if he could do a favor to repay her for—in large part—rescuing him last night. "I could make a donation to your class or host the school's Christmas party at the bar, free of charge. What do you want?"

She stared at him for several long moments, the air between them growing thick and hot. She cleared her throat and said clearly, "I'd like to have an affair with you."

Then she was gone, the door clicking shut behind her. And David was left staring after her, wondering if the whole thing had been some kind of bizarre dream.

Chapter Three

"You asked him to hit the sheets?" Melody let out a hoot of laughter. "Who are you and what have you done with my friend Erin?"

Erin kept her palms pressed tight against her cheeks, willing her face to stop burning. "Oh my gosh," she repeated for the tenth time since she'd climbed in Melody's minivan and told her friend how she'd left things with David. "I'm nobody. I'm delusional. He's going to think I'm crazy. Maybe I *am* crazy."

"You're not crazy." Melody reached out and gently pulled Erin's hands away from her face. "But did you ever think of asking him out on a date?"

"Clearly I wasn't thinking at all." Erin shook her head. "And of course I didn't ask him for a date. David McCay would never go out with someone like me."

"Bargaining for sex seemed like a better idea?"

Erin groaned. "Oh my gosh."

"Why wouldn't he go out with you? You're cute. You're nice. You have decent teeth."

"Decent teeth? My best friend thinks one of my top three selling points is decent teeth? This is even worse than I thought."

Melody laughed softly. "Suzie and I saw the way he looked at you at the bar last night. It was kind of hot."

"The way he looks at a parking meter is hot. That's David. He's not for me. We both know he's not for me."

Her friend didn't deny it, and Erin wasn't sure whether to feel justified or hurt by the silent validation.

"Then why make your little request?"

Erin thought about how she'd felt with David watching her across the small apartment. The way she'd seemed to come alive when he'd placed his hand on the small of her back. The longing for something more in her life.

"He asked me what I wanted and my mouth formed the words before my brain could catch up. He *is* what I want. Not forever. Not for real. But the chance to be with him..."

Melody sighed. "Can you imagine?"

For Erin, fantasizing about David was akin to fangirling over a comic book superhero played by some hot Australian actor on the big screen—larger than life. He was so handsome he took her breath away, but was a whole galaxy out of her league.

He'd probably even look darn good in tights. Erin giggled at the thought, and the fact that she *had* asked him for an affair. What had she been thinking?

"I want to be seen," she said softly. "I'm tired of being invisible."

"We see you," Melody answered. "The kids see you."

"They see Ms. MacDonald. For a school year. Then we have kindergarten graduation and they move on. They grow up. They aren't *mine*." She took another breath. "It's the same reason I'm working with Olivia Travers at the community center on the Crimson Kidzone project."

"You're comparing starting an after-school program for at-risk kids to sleeping with the town hottie?"

"Yes." Erin shook her head. "No. I mean, not when you put it like that. But Kidzone will belong to me. I can make a lasting difference in this community."

"You do that already. That's what being a good teacher is all about. Elaina loves you."

"She's a great kid, but you know that already." Melody's daughter, Elaina, was in Erin's class this year and was the same mix of sweet and spunky as her mother.

"Takes after her dad," Melody said with a wink. Melody had two young kids and a husband who worked long hours as one of Cole Bennett's deputies to provide for his family.

She pulled to a stop at the curb in front of Erin's apartment building. Erin had lived in her apartment in the converted redbrick Victorian since she'd moved back to Crimson after college. All of her furniture was hand-me-downs from her mother. She had white walls and a shower that never got hot enough and it was all…adequate.

"I want to do more, Mel. I want to *be* more. Average has always been enough for me, but sometimes I want more than an ordinary life."

"David McCay sure isn't average."

Erin smiled. "It was a stupid request, and I'll have to apologize. Or maybe he'll pretend it never happened and save us both a lot of embarrassment."

"Is that what you want?"

"It's what I *should* want. I didn't help him last night because I expected anything in return. Rhett's a special kid, but it's clear his life hasn't been easy. He definitely has some behavioral issues, but we were making progress in class. He was responding to me. I don't want him to slip through the cracks."

"Don't take it back, Erin. How many women like us get a chance with someone who looks like that?"

"Says the woman with a ridiculously handsome husband."

"I love Grant to distraction, but we're already a boring married couple. Let me live vicariously through you and your little adventure. I vaguely remember what it was like to be single and playing the field."

"You and Grant started dating when we were juniors in high school."

Melody rolled her eyes. "I said vaguely."

"I need to shower and get ready." Erin opened the car door, the morning breeze tickling the hair that had come loose from the ponytail she wore almost every day. "It's going to be a long one. I'm meeting Olivia at the community center after school to finalize the details on the outreach program."

Melody leaned over the console as Erin hopped out of the car. "At least reassure me that this business with your hottie brewer has nothing to do with the jerk ex-boyfriend."

"Nothing at all," Erin confirmed, and shut the door behind her, never revealing that the fingers of her other hand were tightly crossed behind her back.

Erin parked around the corner from the Crimson Community Center later that afternoon and kept her head down as she moved along the bustling sidewalk. Growing up, Crimson had been nothing more than a sleepy mountain town, always in the shadow of nearby Aspen, which felt to Erin like the more glamorous and showy older sister.

But in recent years, Crimson had come into its own,

attracting new residents and an influx of visitors who appreciated the town's laid-back vibe and the myriad outdoor fun available in the mountains surrounding it.

Now the town was busy most weekends, even though the summer crowds had dispersed and they had a good two months before ski season kicked off.

She'd managed to avoid David at both drop-off and pickup today, although she'd pulled Rhett aside during reading groups after she'd watched the boy purposely knock a bin of markers to the floor, then blame the mess on Elaina Cross, who sat next to him. At first he'd refused to speak or even make eye contact when she'd brought him into the hallway. Eventually he blinked away tears and told her his mommy was going away to a place that would make her better and he had to stay with his uncle David.

Wrapping Rhett in a tight hug, Erin had reassured him that both his mother and his uncle loved him. She'd cautiously brought up the previous night and they'd talked a little about his fears and how important it was for him to feel safe.

While she couldn't avoid David forever, a little distance might work to Erin's advantage. A fierce war was raging between her brain, which wanted the whole embarrassing situation to disappear, and the rest of her body, which was singing the "Hallelujah" chorus at the mere thought that David might agree to her outrageous request.

Erin had been with one and a half men in her lifetime. Well, two men to be exact, but she only counted the first as a half because he'd gotten so drunk during their date that he'd fallen asleep kissing her. Talk about a blow to the ego, and her ego hadn't been much of a force in the first place. But the jerk ex-boyfriend Melody had referred to was the final nail in Erin's confidence coffin.

She and Greg Dellinger had dated for six months, and

their relationship was fine. *Fine*. That should have been her clue to run away as fast as she could. She'd watched enough rom-coms to know that falling in love was supposed to be better than *fine*.

It had been Greg who'd broken up with her, blissfully explaining that he'd fallen in love with a woman who was beautiful, sexy and exciting. Tacitly implying that Erin was none of those things. Not a big shock, but it stung.

Maybe she owed Greg a thank-you, though, because it had been while reevaluating her life—halfway through a carton of Chunky Monkey—that Erin decided she wanted more.

Deserved more.

Changing up her love life was a daunting project, so she'd started her be-more-than-ordinary makeover by contacting Olivia Travers. Ever since she was a girl, Erin had wanted to be a teacher—to help kids learn but also give them a chance to discover all their potential and coax it out.

The same way she'd wished for someone in her life to notice her. With Crimson's ever-expanding population and changing demographics, she was afraid that the neediest kids in the community were getting overlooked. Lost in the shuffle or with families that didn't want the stigma of coming forward for assistance.

Olivia, who'd founded the community center two years ago, had the best of intentions but funding was often difficult to come by for free programming. Erin had outlined her plan for Crimson Kidzone, scheduled a meeting and pitched her idea, offering to volunteer her time to start the program and also work on grant writing to gain additional support.

Her friends at school had encouraged her, while her mom wondered why she'd want to spend more time with children than she already had to for her job. Maureen Mac-Donald was a quiet, keep-to-herself type of woman. She loved Erin and had done her best after Erin's father died of a sudden heart attack when she was in kindergarten. But Maureen dedicated more of her time to her psychology practice than she did to motherhood, and she and Erin had little other than genetics in common. Her mother was content to remain in her introverted bubble and that's how she'd raised her only daughter.

Erin was stepping out of that bubble, even if the encounter with David made her want to jump right back into it.

Her nerves disappeared as soon as she walked into the community center. Her personal life might be a hot mess, but she knew in her heart that the after-school project would be a success. She wouldn't settle for anything less.

Olivia was waiting at the reception desk for her, a chubby-cheeked baby cradled in her arms.

"I hope you don't mind an audience for our meeting," she said apologetically. "The babysitter called in sick."

"Any opportunity to get my dose of snuggles." Erin shifted her backpack so she could reach for baby Molly, who was the most scrumptious five-month-old she'd ever seen.

The little girl was a perfect mix of her mom and dad. She had eyes the same striking green as her mother's. But instead of Olivia's dark hair, she was a towheaded baby with wispy blond hair the same color as Logan Travers's, Molly's doting daddy. Erin wasn't part of the Traverses' wide social circle, but she'd seen the group of friends around town enough to know that Logan, while big and brawny on the outside, was absolute putty in his daughter's hands.

"You're a natural with kindergartners *and* babies," Olivia said as she transferred her daughter to Erin. Coming from Olivia, who was naturally beautiful and had the gentle spirit to match, Erin was grateful to receive the compliment. "Did you grow up in a big family?"

A little pang of disappointment passed through Erin as she shook her head and pressed a kiss to the baby's soft forehead. "I'm an only child, but I always thought it would be fun to have a big family. I love babies."

"You were meant to be a mother."

The other woman's words made something go soft and melty in Erin's heart. She wanted to be a mother, to have someone—or even better, multiple someones—to call her own. The thought of a baby with David McCay's big blue eyes made her chest flutter.

"I have a gut feeling," Olivia continued, "just like I did when you contacted me about the after-school program." She leaned in closer. "Any potential suitors or shall I put the word out? I've learned to trust my instincts."

"Praise the Lord for your instincts," a deep voice said, "or you never would have taken a chance on me." Erin glanced over her shoulder to see Olivia's husband, Logan, standing right behind her. And next to him…David McCay.

Molly let out a little squeak as Erin squeezed a bit too tightly. She rocked the baby and Molly immediately grinned and tugged on the ends of Erin's hair.

"That's right," Olivia said, leaning into her husband when he moved around Erin and draped an arm across her shoulders. "Can you blame me for wanting everyone to be as happy?"

"I'm happy," Erin whispered, even though it wasn't quite the truth. She could feel David's eyes on her, and although she didn't meet his gaze, the intensity of his stare made the hair stand up on the back of her neck.

"How about you, David?" Olivia lifted a brow. "You're single, right?"

"Yep," came the rumbly answer.

Olivia smiled. "Crimson is the perfect place to find true love."

"David is here to talk about the beer for Oktoberfest," Logan said, dropping a kiss on the top of Olivia's head. "Although I'm sure he appreciates your matchmaking efforts."

Erin risked a glance at David, who shrugged. Suddenly she was terrified he might reveal what she'd asked him. It was crazy, but she couldn't stop the fear coursing through her. He opened his mouth but before he could answer, she blurted out the first thing that came to mind, even though it was an obvious lie. "I've got a boyfriend."

Olivia looked disappointed. "Well, I guess I wasn't meant to be a matchmaker after all."

"We'll have to find other ways to keep you busy," Logan said.

"Right now, Erin and I need to go over the last-minute details for her after-school outreach project. The program starts Monday." She scooped the baby out of Erin's arms and handed her to Logan. Molly gurgled happily, curling a fist in the soft denim of her daddy's shirt.

Olivia moved toward the hallway that led to the community center's classrooms. "You coming, Erin?"

Erin realized she was staring at the baby, her arms strangely empty without the lotion-scented bundle. "Right." She darted a glance at David, who arched a brow in response.

One small brow arch she felt all the way to her toes.

An imaginary boyfriend. That should end things before they even got started.

Forcing a smile, she looked from David to Logan. “See you both later,” she called, and hurried after Olivia, ignoring the regret that surged through her as she walked away.

Chapter Four

David waited outside the community center's front door, watching groups of people take to the streets of Crimson on this beautiful fall Friday night. The temperature was quickly cooling, typical at altitude once the sun dipped behind the majestic peak of Crimson Mountain to the town's west.

He imagined the crowds heading toward Elevation for a drink with friends, a reminder that he should be tending bar tonight. He'd been lucky with the brewery, opening just as the picturesque mountain town was hitting a resurgence and having a knack with brewing the ever-popular craft beers.

But he didn't take his success for granted. After destroying his baseball career thanks to one night of reckless stupidity, he'd learned to work hard for what he wanted. He should be working now. Or checking in with Jenna, who was spending the night with Rhett in his loft before they drove to Denver tomorrow to put her on the plane headed for the rehab center in Arizona.

He should be a dozen places that didn't involve standing in the shadows waiting for Erin. David was long past the days of making stupid choices when it came to women, and he'd never had any interest in the type who looked as wholesome as a tall glass of milk.

The door opened and Erin walked out, and all the reasons David shouldn't be waiting for her disappeared under the relentless drumming of need pulsing through his body. He might not understand his reaction to the beautiful schoolteacher, but neither could he ignore it.

"Tell me about the boyfriend," he said, stepping out to block her path.

She stumbled back a step, pressing her hand to her cheek. "Holy cow! You scared the pants off me."

David felt his mouth curve at that. If only.

"No one says *holy cow* in real life," he muttered, reaching out a hand to steady her.

She shrugged off his touch. "Clearly people do say *holy cow*," she countered. "Because I just did." She crossed her arms over a chest that could benefit from a low-cut blouse. Oh, yes. David would definitely like to see this woman in something far more revealing than the conservative pastel-colored shirts she seemed to favor.

The thought of undoing a few of her buttons made his blood run alarmingly hot.

"Why are you skulking around out here?"

"I'm not skulking," he told her. "I'm waiting for you. You were just about to explain why you asked me for sex when you have a boyfriend."

Her delicate brows winged up. "No, I wasn't." She glanced over her shoulder. "Keep your voice down. I don't want anyone to hear..." Even in the waning light he could see color flood her cheeks. When was the last time he'd been around a woman who actually blushed?

"That you propositioned me?" he supplied.

"Stop," she said on a hiss of breath. "It wasn't like that."

"It sure sounded like that to me. But I guess you need to keep me your dirty little secret since there's a *boyfriend* in the picture." He tapped a finger on his chin, as if pondering the concept. "I've never been a kept man before. I'll admit it has a certain appeal."

Her eyes narrowed. "You're teasing me."

He didn't bother to hide his grin. "You seem unfamiliar with the concept."

She stared at him a moment longer, then gave a small sigh. He could almost feel on his skin the puff of breath that left her lips. Damn, but he wanted to feel it. He wanted to taste her to gauge for himself whether she was as sweet as she looked. He eased closer to her, slowly, as if she might spook if he moved too fast.

He'd meant to confront her, demand what the hell she'd been thinking when she'd made that shocking request. But he liked the easy banter they fell into far too much. His life had never been easy, and a bit of innocent flirting with Erin gave him a few minutes' reprieve from all the things he couldn't control.

She bit down on her lip but didn't shy away. He liked that, too. "I don't have a boyfriend," she mumbled.

"Really?" he asked, even though he'd guessed as much.

"Olivia was intent on playing matchmaker, and I didn't want you to be forced into asking me out or anything. That's a horrible feeling and I'm not..."

"Interested?" He chuckled. "We both know that's not true."

A shadow clouded her gaze, and he wasn't sure what he'd said wrong, but he wanted to kick himself for it.

"I'm not your type," she said through clenched teeth, coming up on her toes and tipping back her head so that he got his wish and felt her breath tickle his chin. Her scent was a mix of cinnamon and sugar, like he imagined a kitchen might smell with a batch of cookies baking in the oven. Warm, inviting and the exact opposite of the cramped galley kitchen in the apartment where he'd grown up.

He was so caught up in his reaction that he almost missed the words she spoke. As it was, by the time he opened his mouth to correct her, she'd brushed past him and was around the corner of the building.

"Erin, wait," he called, but instead of slowing she moved faster. It only took a few strides to catch up to her.

"I need to go," she said, keeping her gaze on the ground in front of her when he blocked her path.

"Why do you think you're not my type?" He was curious to know whether her reasons matched his.

She gave a little shake of her head.

"Erin."

"Am I your type?" she asked suddenly, her honey-colored gaze slamming into his.

He opened his mouth, shut it again. How was he supposed to answer that? When she made to move around him again, he settled for the truth.

"You're way too good for me."

The comment earned him an eye roll. "If you say the words *it's me, not you*, I'm going to punch you."

"I'm guessing you don't go around punching people."

"You make me want to start."

He laughed again. "How is it that I'm the bad guy right now?"

"You're not," she whispered. "I should never have made

the request. I was tired, and it was stupid and embarrassing. Can we just forget about it?"

He wished he could. Getting involved with this woman—in any capacity other than as his nephew's teacher—was sure to be trouble for both of them. Why couldn't he make himself walk away?

"No one," he said softly, unable to resist stepping into her space again, "would have to force a man to ask you out."

It was her turn to laugh, but there was no humor in it. All the light was gone from her golden eyes, and he wanted nothing more in life at that moment than to reignite it. "I know who I am, David."

He lifted his hands to cup her cheeks and felt a slight shiver pass through her. It drove him crazy with need. "Take another look," he said, and touched his lips to hers.

Erin's eyes drifted closed even as her body opened like the petals of a flower unfurling in the warm sunshine. Take another look? She'd planned to hold on to this moment like a priceless piece of art. If she could she'd frame it and hang it on her wall so she could always remember.

David McCay was kissing her, and quite thoroughly at that. His lips were soft but firm as they glided over hers and she couldn't resist darting her tongue into his mouth. He rewarded that bit of bravery with a small groan, which made sparks dance across her skin. She leaned into him, her breath hitching when his fingers laced through her hair and tugged gently.

A whistle from a passing car made her wrest away from his embrace. She squeezed her hands into fists and pressed them to her sides when all she wanted was to wrap herself around him and hang on for dear life.

"Women like you don't do PDAs on the sidewalk," he said, his voice rougher than normal.

She bit down on the inside of her cheek and looked up at him through her lashes. "I don't make it a habit," she admitted. The truth was she'd never before had the opportunity. But it was Friday night and it wouldn't be good for one of her students or another teacher to catch her in a full-blown make-out session on a public sidewalk.

"Too good for me," David repeated, and Erin realized he'd actually meant the words when he'd said them earlier.

Her ex had said something similar when he'd broken up with her, but the insinuation behind the comment had been quite different. *Good* had been another way of saying *boring*. But if the heat in David's gaze was any indication, he didn't find her the least bit boring.

Erin's long-suffering ego broke out into a little happy dance, but she quickly pulled the plug on the music. "That isn't true," she said, pressing a hand to lips still tingling from his kiss.

"You asked me for an affair, sweetheart." He smoothed a loose strand of hair away from her face. "Not a date. We both know what that means."

"Would you have gone out on a date if I'd asked?"

He shook his head, and she tried to ignore the pang of disappointment that snaked through her.

"You're a white-picket-fence girl. America and apple pie. What you saw at my sister's apartment pretty much sums up how I was raised. I come from that world. It's what I know."

Right now that didn't matter. This man had flirted with her, then kissed her senseless. Twenty minutes with David had been more exciting than the sum total of the rest of her life. Heck no, she couldn't have an affair with him, even if he was willing. She was liable to spontaneously combust. It was time to get the subject back to safer ground.

"How's Rhett doing?" she asked, reaching into her purse for her keys. She moved to the edge of the sidewalk where her Subaru hatchback was parked at the curb.

"He's with his mom tonight. They're staying at my loft."

"Is your sister okay with going into treatment?"

He nodded. "Deep in her heart she doesn't want to repeat the mistakes our mother made. I have to believe last night was a wake-up call for her."

"Then maybe it was a blessing in disguise. I hope she gets the help she needs." She hit the remote start on her key fob.

"I hope Rhett and I survive the next month together." He ran a hand over his jaw and the scratching sound made her want to whimper. She was truly pathetic.

"He's welcome at Crimson Kidzone in the afternoon. It starts Monday at four. Sign him up if you need a break."

When he stared at her, she held out a hand. "No strings attached or indecent proposals from me. Promise."

He took her hand but instead of shaking it, pressed a lingering kiss on her knuckles. "That would be a huge disappointment."

Erin sighed. Cue the weak knees. "You don't mean that," she whispered.

"I might have enough willpower to leave you alone, but that doesn't mean I won't be thinking about how good we could be together."

He released her hand and she clutched it against her stomach, feeling ridiculously like a teenage girl who wanted to hold on to the imprint of that kiss. "Good to know," she told him.

He winked at her. "Night, Erin. Sweet dreams."

* * *

"Seriously, McCay? Your nephew's kindergarten teacher?"

David blew out a breath at the annoyance in the feminine voice behind him.

He hoisted a bushel of hops over his shoulder and turned. "I don't know what you're talking about, Tracie, but I promised Rhett I'd take him fishing after thirty minutes of screen time so I need to make the most of my electronic babysitter."

It was early Sunday morning—too early considering David hadn't gotten to sleep until after 3:00 a.m. He'd paid one of the waitresses to babysit his nephew last night, which had left him short-staffed since his best—if mouthiest—bartender Tracie Sheldon had taken the evening off for a date with the local orthopedic surgeon who'd been asking her out for months.

Tracie stood behind him now, wearing running shorts and a long-sleeved athletic shirt. Her short blond hair stuck out from under a bright pink headband and he guessed she'd stopped into the bar in the middle of her daily five-mile run.

"Besides, shouldn't you be busy basking in post-date glow or doing the walk of shame or something?"

"I'm not that kind of girl," she shot back, then added softly, "anymore. Besides, it wasn't a good match."

With a quiet sigh, David dropped the heavy bag to the floor. "Why not? Your doctor has bellied up to the bar several nights a week for the past month, even when he's on call and drinking root beer. We might serve up a helluva plate of chicken wings and some crazy good nachos, but there's only so much bar food a man can take."

He leaned in closer. "Unless he has another compelling reason for becoming a regular."

"Compelling." Tracie snorted. "Right. He's a surgeon, Davey, my boy. I'm a high-school dropout bartender. We have nothing in common."

"I've spent some time talking to Luke Baylor. He's a decent guy, Tracie. Worked his way through med school. You work hard, and you're not a high-school dropout anymore. It won't be long until you graduate nursing school. You should hold your head high."

"So tell me about the schoolteacher," she countered, placing her hands on her hips.

"I don't know what you've heard, but there's nothing to tell."

"Do you like her?"

"Do you like Doc Luke?"

She arched a brow. "We had dinner at Carlo's Bistro last night. Remember Lance who washed dishes here for a while?"

"Yeah." David nodded. "Punk kid."

"That's the one. He's a busboy at Carlo's and was all too happy to stop me on the way to the restroom and report he saw you and a dark-haired librarian type sucking face on the street."

David felt a headache begin to pulse behind one temple. "No one was sucking face."

"I figured it was the teacher after seeing the way she looked at you Thursday night. Like she was a kid in a candy store and you were her favorite flavor."

He didn't want to admit how much he liked the idea of that. "You're changing the subject."

"You started it."

"We're quite a pair." He wrapped an arm around the tiny blonde's shoulders—she barely came to his chest—and pulled her in for a hug. "I'm not going to stop trying to make you believe you deserve some happiness."

"Goes both ways," she said, and gently elbowed him in the ribs.

He grunted and squeezed her shoulders. "Rhett's happiness is what matters to me now."

At that moment, Rhett gave a small shout. "Ms. MacDonald," he yelled, and scrambled out of the booth, his iPad forgotten on the table.

Tracie took a step away from him as David turned to see Erin, backlit in the doorway of the bar by the morning sunlight. Her dark jeans hugged her curves and a cranberry-colored sweater with a scooped neckline made her skin look even more luminous. It was difficult to read her expression, but her gaze was bouncing between him and Tracie in a way David didn't like one bit.

"Don't just stand there staring," Tracie muttered. "Go to her. I'm going to slip out through the kitchen."

"Tracie, you don't need to..." David started, but he was talking to her back.

"Ms. MacDonald, I live in a bar now." David cringed as Rhett's voice carried across the empty space.

"We don't live in the bar," David corrected as he moved forward. *Go to her*, Tracie had said. What he wanted to do was swing her into his arms and bury his nose against the crook of her neck. Her thick hair was pulled back into another ponytail.

Did she ever wear it down? Right now he would give just about anything to see it falling in waves over her shoulders. He'd been too long without a woman if he was now obsessing over Erin's hair.

"I know," she answered. "You have a loft upstairs. I didn't mean to interrupt." Her gaze traveled past him to where Tracie had disappeared. "I was heading to the bakery and your door was open..."

"You're not interrupting," he said quickly, coming to

stand behind his nephew. "Tracie works here, and she stopped by after her run. She had a date last night." She bit down on her lip and he quickly added, "With someone else. Not me. We're not…" He raked a hand through his hair. "She's a friend. The guy she went out with is a doctor. A surgeon. He—"

"Uncle David, why are you talking so fast?" He glanced down to find Rhett staring up at him, then raised his gaze to Erin's. He was babbling. He'd never babbled in his entire life.

She flashed a shy smile. "I'm going to grab breakfast at Life Is Sweet, then head over to the community center to set up a few things for tomorrow. I thought Rhett might like to help me if it's okay with you."

He felt Rhett fidget against his legs. "What do you think, buddy? We can head to the river a little later if you want to help Ms. MacDonald."

"I might mess things up," Rhett said, kicking the toe of one ratty sneaker against the scuffed wood floor. "I have to stay out of the way around here."

David sighed. He'd said those words this morning—pre-coffee—when he'd set up Rhett with the iPad.

"You won't mess up anything." Erin crouched down in front of the boy. "In fact, some of the supplies I'm using are way back in a closet and I need someone small enough to crawl in and push them out to me."

Rhett nodded. "I can do that."

"Then we've got a deal." She straightened, and David expected to see censure in her big eyes, but instead they were gentle in a way that made his heart hammer in his chest.

"Can I go in my pj's?" Rhett asked.

Erin smiled. "This might be a good time to get dressed for the day. Can you do that?"

"Me and Ruffie have a bedroom upstairs." He pointed to the raggedy blue dog sitting on the booth where he'd been playing a video game. "He gets nervous when we're not together."

"He's welcome to come with us," Erin offered.

"Yeah," Rhett agreed. "He'd like that."

He ran to the table, grabbed the dog and then headed for the hallway leading to the staircase that accessed the upper floor. There was also an entrance off the street, but David used the one that led directly into his office in the back of the bar when things weren't busy.

"I suck at this," he mumbled when Rhett was out of sight. "Jenna hasn't even been gone twenty-four hours and Rhett feels like he's in the way."

"It's a big change for both of you. How did it go yesterday?"

"Jenna cried. Rhett cried. He was sullen all day yesterday, and the first thing he asked this morning is when she's coming home. I felt like a total ass for arranging her stay in rehab. Maybe she could get clean and still be here, you know?"

"It's not long in the grand scheme of things and could make a real difference. That would make everything worth it. A kid deserves to grow up feeling safe. Your sister is lucky to have you to step in and help her. You're giving both of them another chance."

He blew out a breath. "How did you know exactly what I needed to hear this morning?"

Color rose to her cheeks. "It's the truth."

It wasn't just the words she spoke that made him feel better. It was the fact that she'd come to check on him. Okay, maybe she'd come to check on Rhett, but David still reaped the benefit. *She* was exactly what he needed. "Thank you."

They stared at each other for several long moments, and the spark of awareness that connected them seemed to shimmer and thrum in the air. It made him want to pull her in and kiss her again, but then he thought of Tracie and the kid who'd reported him Friday night. Normally, David didn't care who saw him doing what, but Erin was different. She was too good to be dragged through any sort of gossip mill, especially when she was starting her new program at the community center.

He crossed his arms over his chest to resist the urge to touch her. "Rhett won't be long." He made his tone purposefully chilly.

Disappointment flashed in her brown eyes before she cocked her head and studied him, as if she was trying to riddle out secrets. "This place is different during the day," she said, moving away from him and trailing her long fingers over the polished mahogany of the bar. He could imagine a lot of other places those fingers should be traveling. Namely all over his damn body.

"The architecture is beautiful." She pointed to the vaulted ceiling, where rough-hewn beams stretched across the open space.

"Logan helped me design it," David said, following her as she moved through the high tables. Following her like a puppy on a leash. Never had he felt so under a woman's spell as he did with Erin. The crazy part was she had no idea the power she had over him.

"Did he do the renovations, too? When I was growing up, this place was a grocery store, then it stood vacant for a number of years."

He'd forgotten that she was a Crimson native. The town was a tight-knit community and everyone seemed to know their neighbors and their neighbors' business. But before Rhett started school, David had never heard of Erin Mac-

Donald. “The building was bank-owned when I bought it. I got a great deal.”

She smiled at him over her shoulder. “You must have had a clear vision.”

“I went to college on a baseball scholarship, but only lasted a couple of years. It sounds crazy now, but I took a brewing lab sciences class freshman year and got hooked on the process. I was good at it, but baseball came first. When I got drafted, the beer brewing moved to the back burner for a few years. I stopped playing ball, but then Jenna needed me out here. I needed a job and had enough money to make the business work.”

“Why did you give up baseball?”

He gave a harsh laugh. “Not exactly my choice. I screwed things up pretty good. Not worth rehashing the details, but suffice it to say it was totally my fault.”

“You do that too much,” she said, moving toward him until she was directly in front of him. “You take the blame for anything that goes bad.”

David felt his eyes narrow. “Only when I deserve it.”

She poked him in the chest. “It seems like you’re of the opinion that you always deserve it.”

He clamped his mouth shut and stared down at her. There was no right way to respond to that. He didn’t always do the wrong thing, but the times he’d messed up in his life had resulted in grim consequences for the people around him.

“You can’t control everything. Sometimes bad stuff happens no matter what you do to prevent it.”

He wrapped his hand around her finger and lowered it. “Other times it can be prevented, and I’ve often failed at that.”

He expected her to wrench out of his grasp, but she

surprised him by gently squeezing his hand. "I wish you saw yourself the way I see you."

David felt her words like a vise clamping around his heart. The ways this woman could wreck him boggled his mind. Pulling away from her, he took several long steps toward the back hallway. "Rhett, you almost ready?" he called up the stairs.

"Coming," the boy shouted as his small feet pounded down the steps. He bounded into the hallway, the ever-present blue dog tucked against his side.

"Shoes, buddy," David said softly. His nephew had a habit of putting his shoes on the wrong feet.

With a sigh, Rhett dropped to the floor and undid the Velcro straps of his superhero sneakers and switched them to the correct feet. David's heart squeezed even harder as Rhett's tongue darted out the corner of his mouth. It meant he was concentrating hard and was the same quirk Jenna'd had as a girl.

David ruffled Rhett's hair as he stood. "Listen to Ms. MacDonald and do what she says," he told the boy. "No trouble."

"Okay."

He turned and looked at Erin, but her attention was focused on Rhett. "I'm glad you're coming with me this morning," she said.

Rhett gave a sharp nod and inched forward.

"I need another hour or so to get things settled here," David told her. "I'll pick him up after that."

"No rush," she answered, but still didn't look at him. "We'll stay busy."

He'd been the one to pull away a few minutes ago, but now the distance separating them seemed wider than simply physical space. It felt like he was losing something that had never belonged to him in the first place. The sensation made him want to throw a tantrum, like a baby whose favorite toy was taken away.

Erin held out her hand to Rhett, and the boy placed his smaller one in it. They walked out the open door and disappeared into the cool autumn morning.

David stood in his empty bar, staring at the dust motes that floated through the rays of sun shining in from the bar's front windows. He'd never minded being alone before. Why did it feel so damn uncomfortable now?

Chapter Five

"I owe you for this morning."

Erin almost stumbled off the end of the fishing dock at the sound of David's voice directly behind her.

He reached out a hand to steady her, but as much as she wanted to lean into his touch, she shrugged it off. Not going there, she reminded herself.

"You don't owe me. I told you I wanted to help with Rhett."

One side of his mouth quirked as he stared at her from behind dark sunglasses. "You also told me—"

"Don't say it." She held up a hand. "We've agreed that request was a moment of sleep-deprived stupidity on my part."

"I haven't agreed to anything." His deep voice once again set off tremors inside her.

"I thought you and Rhett were going to look for rocks to skip."

David gestured to where the boy was busily digging in the sand and gravel that made up the shoreline of Crimson Reservoir. “He got distracted.”

She smiled as she watched Rhett, crouched low and with his too-long hair hanging over one eye, his attention completely focused on his task. “This is good for him, David. He needs some time to just be a kid in nature.”

“This place can make anyone feel better.”

She lifted her gaze to take in the awe-inspiring scenery around them. They were standing on the east side of the seven-mile-wide reservoir situated about thirty minutes outside of town. Rhett had insisted she accompany them on their planned fishing trip when David came to pick him up at the community center.

She should have said no. It had been a spontaneous decision to make the boy part of her morning on her way to the bakery earlier. A good decision, she thought, because both Rhett and David had looked grateful and relieved at her offer. But spending too much time with David was dangerous for her emotional health.

She’d spent far too much time since Friday replaying their kiss in her head. Instead of satisfying her, it had made her want more, even though she knew she shouldn’t.

This afternoon only heightened her need. Having a crush on David was one thing, but watching his patience with Rhett and how hard he was trying to connect with the boy made Erin like him on an entirely different level. Once Rhett got tired of fishing, he’d gone to play on the shore, leaving David and Erin together on the dock.

Sunlight sparkled on the water, and a breeze made the changing aspen leaves flutter and sing around them. The breathtaking view of Crimson Mountain on the far side of the water made the reservoir one of the most beautiful places she'd ever seen. It seemed funny now that she'd never come out here before.

Her mom hadn't been much for outdoor activities. Erin knew kids came to the lake to hang out in high school, big groups or on dates. She was pretty sure the scenic overlook they'd passed on the way to the parking lot was still a popular make-out spot for teens in town. But she'd never been part of that crowd.

Now she wished she had been.

"I'd give way more than a penny to read your thoughts right now." David bent and picked up the fishing pole that he'd left next to her on the dock.

"I was thinking about what I still need to do to be ready for tomorrow," she lied.

"That makes you blush?"

She pressed her hands to her cheeks. "I'm not blushing."

He chuckled. "Want to throw in a line yourself? All you've gotten to do so far is watch me teach Rhett to fish."

"He likes it out here. Outside. Sitting in a classroom all day is tough for boys, and a lot of them go home and spend the rest of the day playing video games or watching TV."

"Like my nephew?"

She shrugged. "I'm sorry. I'm not trying to criticize your sister."

"It's fine," David answered, his voice tight. "Just because I moved to Crimson to help doesn't mean I knew how to or that Jenna wanted me involved. I should have been paying more attention. She was hiding things from me. Turns out Rhett was alone a lot more than I realized. He's pretty addicted to his screen time."

"Then today is even more of a treat for him."

David stepped closer, and she could see the shadow across his jaw that meant he hadn't shaved that morning.

He wore faded jeans and an olive-colored T-shirt with the Elevation Brewery logo across the front. Everything about him fascinated her.

"So you gonna do some fishing?"

"I don't know how," she answered, but took the thin pole he held out to her. "I mean, I was listening when you showed Rhett but..."

"I'll give you a lesson, too." He grasped her shoulders and turned her so she was facing the water. Then he moved to stand behind her, his body touching hers from chest to thigh. A crazy buzzing started in her head, and she swallowed back the little whimper that rose in her throat.

"Hold the pole so your two middle fingers are on either side of the reel," he said, his breath warm against her neck.

She tightened her grasp on the fishing pole and heard him chuckle. "Not in a death grip. Firm but not too tight."

She choked back a laugh because it sounded a lot like he was instructing her on something other than fishing. "Okay," she whispered.

"Hold the line against the rod with your index finger and flip the bail with your other hand." He guided her hand to the narrow piece of metal. "Give the line some slack and we're going to bring the rod back and cast."

Her mind was reeling, but she tried to follow his directions. With a shaking finger, she flipped the bail, drew the pole over her head and cast. The line spun, then the bobber dropped with a *plop* into the water only a foot in front of the dock.

"I can't do this," she whispered, trying to hand the pole back to David and move away.

"You can," he said, and tightened his hold on her. He took the rod from her, his arms reaching around her, and reeled in the line. "The motion comes from your wrist and hand, not your shoulder. Now take a breath."

She did and was immediately overwhelmed by the scent of soap and mint gum with the irresistible essence of David thrown in for good measure. It was different from kissing him, of course, but no less intimate. Erin struggled to keep her reaction to him hidden. "I've lived my whole life without learning to fish," she told him. "I can probably manage without the skill."

"Not on my watch," he said, and wrapped her hand around the pole once again. "You're going to catch a fish today."

Erin forced another breath and concentrated on not freaking out any more than she already was. Her goal for the year had been stepping out of her comfort zone, and today definitely counted. She glanced over her shoulder to see Rhett still focused on his rock and stone collection on the bank. "I don't know about a fish," she murmured. "I'll be satisfied if I throw this thing in the water without embarrassing myself."

"It's called casting a line," David said against her ear. His lips brushed the sensitive skin just below her earlobe.

A shiver ran through her in response, and she gripped the fishing pole more tightly. "I can't focus when you do that."

"Then you should stop being so sexy."

She grunted out a laugh at that. Erin was a lot of things, but sexy had never been one of them. The reminder was enough to help her rein in her foolish desire for this man. She couldn't help but think this was another part of his thank-you to her for helping with Rhett. Have a little flirtatious pity on the boring schoolteacher.

She squeezed her eyes shut for a moment and tried to compose herself. He was a man. She was a woman. They were fishing while his nephew—her student—played nearby. A casual afternoon. No need to read more into it than that.

"Tell me what to do again," she told him when she'd pulled herself together.

He repeated the instructions and she followed them, letting out a small cry of delight when the fishing line sailed through the air to land a respectable fifty feet out in the lake.

"I did it," she whispered.

"Now reel it in again," David said.

She did and the zip of the spinning reel was the best thing she'd heard in a long time. She cast twice more, the feel of the rod in her hand more natural with every moment.

"I think you've got it."

She realized David was still standing directly behind her only when he moved away. Her body wanted to protest, but she was too excited about her newfound skill at casting.

"I like it," she told him.

"We'll move to fly-fishing next," he answered with a slow smile. "I'd like to see you in a pair of waders."

Before she could react, the orange bobber floating on top of the water disappeared and she felt a hard tug on the line.

"A fish!" Rhett yelled at the top of his lungs as he ran toward them.

"Reel it in," David shouted as the line made a fast whirring sound.

With a squeak, Erin grabbed the spinning handle of the reel and began to turn it counterclockwise toward her body.

David was behind her again a moment later, his hand steadying her arm.

"Pull the rod against your body," he commanded. "You'll get more leverage."

"Take it," she said in a rush of breath. "I can't—"

"Yes, you can."

"You're doing it, Ms. MacDonald," Rhett said excitedly when he got to her side. He tugged on the hem of her shirt. "Don't let it get away."

"Keep going," David told her, his voice gentler. "You've got this."

Erin felt a grin split her face as she continued to bring the fish closer to the dock. David disappeared for a moment, then reappeared a minute later with a net in one hand.

"Bring him in, sweetheart," he said as he knelt at the edge of the dock.

The fish surfaced and struggled in the water, fighting hard against the hook that tethered him to her line. The sound of splashing broke the quiet of the lake as the water rippled and churned around the fish.

"He's so cute." Rhett crouched down next to David. "He's a boy, right?"

"Hard to tell right now." David grabbed the line, then scooped the net into the water. When it emerged again, the fish was in it, its gills opening and closing in the unfamiliar air.

"I don't want to kill him," Erin said, suddenly having a rush of sympathy for the little creature.

"It'll be fine," David assured her. "Hold the net, Rhett."

"Got it." The boy grabbed the handle with two hands while David removed the fish from the net. He pulled a tool out of his pocket and stuck it into the fish's mouth, extracting the hook.

Then he turned and presented the creature to Erin. "Here you go."

She placed the rod onto the dock and stepped forward. "It's so pretty." She traced one finger over the fish's pink-tinged side.

"It's a rainbow trout," David told her. "Hand Rhett your phone and take the fish. We'll get a photo before we throw him back."

"Or her," Erin said. "He could be a she."

"Yeah, but I don't think you want to cut her open and look for an egg sack."

"No." Erin made a face at the same time Rhett shouted, "Yes!"

She took her phone from her pocket, flipped it to camera mode and handed it to Rhett.

"Hold on tight," David advised as he passed the fish to her.

She didn't have time to think about whether she actually wanted her hands on the slimy, slippery creature before it was in them.

Despite the fact that she was slightly grossed out by holding a fish, she smiled when David took the phone from the boy and snapped her photo.

"Now throw it back," he told her and she flipped the fish into the reservoir. There was a splash, and the fish shimmered on the surface for a few seconds before swimming off.

"Bye, fish," Rhett called, then glanced up at David. "Can we skip stones now?"

"Sure, buddy. We'll collect the fishing gear and head over to you."

"I'll get more ready." Rhett smiled, then walked back toward his rock pile.

"I held a fish," Erin murmured, still holding her arms out in front of her.

"Like a pro," David confirmed. He pulled a bandanna

out of the pocket of his cargo pants and took her hand in his, gently wiping each of her fingers.

"I'm going to need to shower for days to get the fish smell off me."

"One hot shower should do the trick," he said with a smile. "If you're looking for a volunteer to scrub your back…"

She yanked her hands away from his. "You shouldn't tease me."

He leaned in and brushed a quick kiss across her lips. "Who says I'm teasing?"

Heat spiked through her, and her whole body flooded with need. As if unaware of her reaction, David simply grabbed the fishing pole and net and walked off the dock toward Rhett on the shore.

She followed, trying to keep her focus on the boy. That's why she was here—to help with Rhett. Anything more would surely end in emotional disaster.

David climbed the front steps of Crimson Elementary the following Wednesday afternoon, cursing himself for believing he finally had his life under control.

After Sunday's fishing excursion, something had changed with Rhett. His nephew had always been a bit distant, as if Jenna had warned him about coming to rely on Uncle David. Although he understood the sentiment, the tacit rejection still stung. But between the fishing lessons and skipping stones across the placid surface of the reservoir, the boy had started to relax and engage with David in a way he hadn't before.

David gave a lot of the credit to Erin. Her presence seemed to bridge the gap that he couldn't manage on his own. Rhett clearly loved having the attention of his teacher outside the classroom. Her easy smile and gentle encouragement softened the boy, and he was far more connected when she was around.

The funny thing was, David felt the exact same way. Despite a long string of girlfriends, he'd never been one for domestication. He was used to tumultuous relationships—loud arguments and intense make-up sessions that he'd assumed were normal given how he was raised.

Everything in his life had been emotional crisis and big scenes. But Erin made the ordinary bits feel just as exciting as the adrenaline rush that came from being swept along in a drama-filled haze.

He hadn't seen much of her since Sunday, despite dropping off and picking Rhett up from school every day and the fact that the boy had spent two afternoons in her after-school program.

It was a relief to have a safe place for Rhett to be in the hours before David could break away from work. He'd hired another bartender so he didn't have to deal with late nights, but with the plans for Oktoberfest and the festival's highly anticipated beer competition well under way, this wasn't a time he could take an extended vacation from the bar.

Between school, Erin and a couple trusted babysitters, David thought he was successfully managing his newfound role of single parent. Then he'd gotten the call from the school's principal, alerting him that Rhett had been in a fight with another boy during recess, the result of which would be a one-day suspension.

Hell, even David had made it to third grade before he'd been suspended for the first time. So much for having things under control.

He was buzzed into the building and headed for the reception desk. The woman behind it glanced up as he approached. She took him in head to toe and he saw her eyes widen. That's when he remembered the T-shirt he was wearing, which had the words I'd Tap That emblazoned across the front.

Way to make an impression.

Rhett's principal was going to love him. David did a mental eye roll as he wondered what Erin would think.

Probably that she'd dodged a bullet when he hadn't immediately taken her up on her offer to have an affair.

A moment later, an older woman with a sleek brown bob and wire-framed glasses came out of the office to greet him.

"Mr. McCay, I'm Karen Henderson, Crimson Elementary's principal."

"Call me David," he said as he shook her hand.

"Thank you for coming in today. I'm sorry we're meeting under these circumstances. I understand from Ms. MacDonald that there have been some disruptions in Rhett's home life recently."

David gritted his teeth as he followed the woman into her office. "Is Rhett okay? Where is he?"

"He'll be along shortly," she said, moving behind her desk and taking a seat. "He's with the school counselor at the moment. I wanted a chance to speak to you first."

The office was just as he remembered the principal's office at the three different elementary schools he'd attended as a kid. His mom had a habit of moving frequently, taking short-term leases on whatever cheap apartment she could get near her latest boyfriend.

"There's no need to sugarcoat it," he told her. "My sister is getting help for her problems. Rhett and I are coping as best we can. You can be sure nothing like today will repeat itself."

She nodded and opened a file on her desk. "I appreciate that, Mr. McCay."

"David."

"The other boy—the one he fought with—is also being disciplined. He's a second grader at the school."

David felt his temper flare. How had Rhett managed to get in a fight with a second grader?

"Why did it happen?" he demanded. "Rhett's only been at the school a month."

She shook her head, her already-thin lips pressing into a tight line. "From what the teachers and I were able to get out of them, the other boy made a disparaging remark about Rhett's mother."

Everything in David went still—only for a second. Then memories from his childhood, of his mother and the fights he got in defending her honor, crashed through him.

"I want to see Rhett," he said through clenched teeth. "And Erin. Where's Erin?"

The principal's shoulders stiffened. "Ms. MacDonald," she said, placing an emphasis on the name as if to remind him of his place, "is out of the building today."

"Out where?"

"At a district-wide training. Rhett's class had a substitute teacher. Mrs. Mills has been a sub at the school for quite a few years, longer than Ms. MacDonald has been here. She's quite capable."

"She's not Erin," he said. At the woman's frown, he added, "Ms. MacDonald. Rhett has a special bond with Ms. MacDonald."

The woman's frown deepened. "Be that as it may, she's his *teacher*, Mr. McCay. Nothing more. Whether it's with Ms. MacDonald or another member of our staff, your nephew is in good hands at our school."

There was a knock at the door, and it opened to reveal another woman who looked to be about ten years younger than the principal. She was petite, with bright red hair and a kind face. "Rhett would like to see his uncle."

Karen Henderson nodded and the door opened wider to reveal Rhett standing next to the redhead.

David stood, not sure where to start with the conflicting emotions simmering inside him.

To his surprise, Rhett launched himself forward and covered the space between them in a few hurried steps. The boy reached out, and David automatically lifted him into his arms. Rhett held tight, his small body shaking as he clung to David.

"It's okay," David whispered, even though it was a lie for both of them. "You're okay."

"We need to talk about the situation," the principal said softly, and Rhett's hold on David tightened even more. "He has to understand—"

"I'll make sure he understands," David said. "Right now, I'm taking him home."

"Mr. McCay—"

"A one-day suspension." David glanced over his shoulder as he moved toward the door. "He'll be back in class on Friday."

He didn't bother to wait for a response. Settling Rhett's weight on his hip, he walked out of the school and toward his truck, which was parked at the curb. "Let's get you buckled in," he said gently, and after a moment Rhett's arms went slack.

"Are you hurt?"

The boy gave a slight shake of his head.

David settled him in the booster seat Jenna had helped him install and strapped him in, the buckle clicking shut.

Rhett kept his head lowered, and David didn't say anything else. He needed to get away from the school and also wanted some time to rein in his emotions. Anger was part of it—some of it aimed at Rhett for getting into the fight in the first place. But most of it was leveled at Jenna, for putting all of them in this situation.

He flipped on the radio as he pulled onto the road, and a raucous country song about whiskey and women who broke a cowboy's heart filled the cab.

It fit his mood perfectly.

Not that his heart was broken. He wasn't fool enough to open himself up to that kind of trouble. But betrayal swept through him nonetheless. He'd so quickly come to rely on Erin—her sweetness and the kindness she'd shown toward Rhett. He'd wanted to believe…that it was more than a sense of duty. Of course she had other responsibilities, and caring for Rhett was part of her job.

He glanced in the rearview mirror and saw Rhett with his head still down, wringing his small hands together in his lap. His chest rose and fell in shallow breaths, as though he was also struggling to hold it together.

David's anger melted away. He still wanted answers from his nephew, and for the boy to understand that fighting at school wouldn't be tolerated. But the kid was hurting and probably felt totally alone in the world. David knew a lot about being alone.

He didn't want that for Rhett.

Downtown Crimson was bustling as he turned the truck onto Main Street. The weather was perfect for the first week of October, still warm with just a hint of cool to the air. High on the mountain, the aspen leaves were changing from green to gold. Soon the riot of color would extend down into town, and the weekends would be busy with fall tourists and a few hunters on their way to higher elevations.

He pulled the truck to a stop against the curb and punched in a quick text to Tracie. He was supposed to have a meeting this afternoon with the head of a regional bottling company to ensure that everything was on track for the Oktoberfest celebration. He was going to have to delegate, even though it killed him to relinquish that kind of control.

He'd catch up later, he told himself. Right now, the more important work was with his nephew.

"This isn't your parking spot." David undid the buckle of the booster seat, and Rhett climbed out of the truck to the sidewalk.

"I thought we'd stop at Life Is Sweet for a cookie on the way home," David told him, pointing to the sign above the bakery a few doors down.

As they walked, Rhett said quietly, "I got in trouble today."

"I know, buddy. That's why I was at the school."

"Do you still want to get me a cookie?" There was a hitch in his voice that made David's chest ache.

"I sure do." David ruffled his hair. "We're going to need to talk about what happened, but I think a snack will make both of us feel better."

"Yeah," Rhett agreed after a moment, and slipped his hand into David's.

The chimes above the door jingled as they walked in. Despite living in Crimson for almost three years, David had only been in the bakery a handful of times. He wasn't much for sweets and didn't drink coffee. Besides, there was something about the cozy feel of the space that made his skin itch with a need he couldn't quite identify.

The woman who owned Life Is Sweet, Katie Crawford, was always friendly and he'd met her husband, Noah, on several occasions.

But a bakery was different from a brewpub. There was

a sense of community that radiated from it, and David had never had a desire to be part of any community.

Yet somehow he knew it was the right thing for Rhett.

Maybe for both of them.

He ordered two chocolate chip cookies and a milk for Rhett, then they took a seat in the small café area at a wrought iron table. There was a young couple at the table next to them, both with steaming coffee mugs in front of them and both tapping away on their phones. David had seen the same thing happen with people in the bar. They came in groups but instead of talking, they spent their time scrolling through social media or dating sites.

It made him feel old at twenty-nine that he wanted no part of online dating. He hadn't even thought about dating since his move to Crimson—at least until he'd met Erin.

With a sigh, he put her out of his mind as best he could and focused on Rhett.

The boy was nibbling the edge of his cookie and had a tiny smear of chocolate at the corner of his mouth.

"A second grader?" David asked casually, figuring the best way to deal with today was to get straight to the point.

Rhett shrugged. "He was only a little bigger than me."

"That's not really the point."

Rhett paused midbite and glanced up. "Mommy said you got in lots of trouble when you were a kid. She told me not to be like you."

David sighed. *Thanks, Jenna.*

"That was probably good advice, but here we are. Want to tell me about the fight?"

Rhett shook his head, his shaggy hair falling across one eye. Add a kid's haircut to the to-do list, David thought.

"We have to talk about it, unless you'd rather go back to the school and talk to Ms. Henderson and your teacher."

"Ms. MacDonald was gone today," Rhett said glumly. "I can't tell her."

Right. Erin hadn't been there to run interference. David knew he had no right to be angry but couldn't seem to stop the feeling of betrayal that washed through him. Erin made him believe he wasn't alone in caring for Rhett. That he had things under control. It was somehow easier to direct his frustration toward her than to any of the other things in his life that seemed beyond his control. "Then tell me."

"He called Mommy a bad word," the boy said, breaking the remainder of his cookie in half. "Real bad."

"What word?"

Rhett scrunched up his nose, as if he'd smelled something rotten. Then he climbed off the chair and moved to David's side. He stood on tiptoe and when David bent toward him, whispered the word *slut* in his ear.

Blood roared in David's head as he stared down at his *five-year-old* nephew. "Do you know what that word means?"

"Isaac said Mommy's boyfriend is his daddy, and she stole him from Isaac's mommy."

David didn't know much about the man his sister had been dating for the past few months. She'd told him he had a good job and they were just having fun together. Either she didn't know or had forgotten to mention that he also had another family. One that was targeting Rhett.

"What's Isaac's last name?"

"I don't know," Rhett answered, climbing back into his seat. "He came up to me when I was on the monkey bars and pushed me and said mean things about Mommy." He gripped the milk bottle tightly. "I got really mad. I didn't mean to get into a fight, Uncle David. Then the teacher came and yelled at me and he cried and she yelled more."

He shook his head. "Ms. MacDonald never yells no matter how mad we make her."

"Ms. MacDonald won't always be there for you, Rhett." David didn't mean for his words to come out harshly, but the boy's bottom lip quivered.

"He shouldn't have said what he did about your mom." David gentled his voice and leaned forward. "Did you explain it to your teacher and the principal?"

Rhett shook his head, and by the set of his jaw David understood why. Rhett was young but still old enough to understand there could be some truth in the other boy's accusations. Not the name-calling. That was inexcusable. But Jenna had a history of making poor choices in men.

Just like David's mother. He'd spent too much of his childhood trying to protect his mom without even realizing he was doing it. Making excuses for why she missed parent-teacher conferences, pretending she was picking him up around the block when in reality he walked home, forging signatures on forms and permission slips every year.

He'd tried to protect Jenna, but in the end he'd failed her.

He wouldn't fail Rhett.

"I'm going to make sure it doesn't happen again," he promised the boy. "But if anyone gives you trouble, talk to a teacher instead of fighting. Talk to me. I'm here to help you, Rhett. It's my job."

"I thought your job was making beer."

David smiled, but the muscles of his face felt stiff. "I do that, too, but nothing is more important to me than you. Nothing."

Chapter Six

Erin walked into Elevation later that night, her eyes scanning the bar for David.

Instead, the gorgeous bartender who'd given her the once-over last Sunday met her gaze.

"He's got the night off," she said as Erin approached.

"I went upstairs and rang the bell," Erin admitted, "but he didn't answer."

"Maybe he doesn't want to talk," the woman said and turned her back on Erin to grab two pint glasses from underneath the shelf behind her. "To you," she added over her shoulder.

Erin felt color rush to her cheeks. She was well aware that David didn't want to talk to her. She'd been trying to get in touch with him since she stopped at the school after her district meeting and Karen Henderson told her what had happened with Rhett on the playground.

The principal had made it quite clear that Erin should

keep her relationship with both Rhett and David professional and not allow herself to become involved in their personal lives.

Smart advice, but Erin's heart was already involved. It killed her to think of the boy in trouble and afraid when she hadn't been there to smooth things over for him.

She stepped up to the bar and waited for the bartender to serve the two beers to the men sitting next to where Erin stood.

"Why don't you pull up a seat and talk to us, darlin'," one of the men, a scruffy-looking guy in a Broncos jersey, said.

Erin swallowed. The only time she'd come to a bar before tonight had been with a group of girlfriends, and no one had paid much attention to her. "Thank you for the offer, but I don't think so." She leaned toward the bar and caught the petite blonde's eye. "I need to see David," she whispered.

"He's no fun anymore," the second man said. "Doesn't live up to his baseball reputation at all."

"Shut up, Donnie," the bartender snapped.

"You know it's true, Tracie," the man shot back. "If half the stories about Dave are true, he got more action than a fox in a chicken coop back in the day."

"Now all he does is work." The first man darted a look at Erin. "No matter how many hot chicks throw themselves at him. We need some excitement around here."

Tracie rolled her eyes, and Erin wasn't sure whether it was in response to the man's complaint about David or the implication that Erin was a "hot chick."

"You'd better not let your wives hear you talking like that," Tracie said.

"Why do you think we want Davey to get some action?"

Donnie took a long pull on his beer. "I don't want trouble at home. But I'm not dead, just married."

The bartender huffed out a laugh and turned away without bothering to acknowledge Erin again.

Erin should give up. David didn't want her, and she could talk to Rhett when he returned to school after the suspension.

Somehow she couldn't force herself to walk away. That was what she'd ordinarily do, but she was done being ordinary.

She stepped behind the bar and followed Tracie down the length of it, tapping the tiny woman on the shoulder when she got close.

"Seriously?" the woman asked as she whirled around. "You can't be back here."

"I need to see him."

"He's used to handling things on his own." Tracie crossed her arms over her chest and glared at Erin. "It's easier that way. No one gets hurt."

Erin was pretty sure the gorgeous bartender wasn't only talking about David. "He doesn't have to do this alone." She made her voice purposefully gentle. "I'm not going to hurt him. I promise."

Tracie studied her for a few seconds, then reached in her pocket and pulled out a set of keys. "The silver one unlocks the office and the staircase inside that leads up to the loft. You'd better make this right. David and Rhett both need that."

Erin had no idea how to make anything right at the moment, but she nodded and took the key ring. "Thank you."

"You're different than you look," Tracie said. "Stronger."

A bit of happiness trickled through Erin at the reluctant compliment. "You're not quite as scary."

Tracie laughed softly. "Don't tell anyone."

Erin closed her hand around the keys and headed through the brewpub. She unlocked the office door and flipped on the light, taking a moment to gather her courage before moving to the wood panel door on the far side. Away from the noise of the bar, every sound seemed amplified and the *click* of the lock as she turned the key reverberated in her ears.

She let herself into the narrow staircase and locked the door behind her, as she had in the office, as well. Before she made it halfway up the stairs, the door at the top opened.

David stared down at her, his expression unreadable with his face concealed by shadows.

"Do you pick locks in your spare time?" he asked.

"Tracie gave me the key," she said, proud that her voice didn't shake. She forced herself to keep moving toward him, even though her knees were practically knocking. As silly as it sounded, it felt like she was going into battle. "You wouldn't return my calls and texts or answer when I knocked."

"Rhett was in the bath."

"I wanted to check on him." She was on the step below him now, gazing up into the hard planes of his face.

"You'll see him when he goes back to school," he said tightly. "Unless there's another sub in his class."

"That's not fair. What happened today isn't my fault."

For a moment she thought he might slam the door in her face, and she wondered what had possessed her to come here in the first place. Maybe her fantasy life had truly taken over and she'd imagined the connection between them. Maybe she was so desperate to be needed by someone that she'd read more into the situation than was really there.

Then he reached out and hauled her against him. His arms wrapped tight around her, and he rested his cheek on the top of her head. She could feel the tension coiled in him, electric and barely contained. And she knew she hadn't imagined any of it. This man needed her, and that understanding made her heart sing.

"You're right. I'm angry at Jenna for putting all of us in this position. I don't mean to take it out on you. I'm sorry."

"Me, too," she answered, speaking into the soft fabric of his shirt. She turned her head so she could feel the warm skin of his throat against the tip of her nose.

He drew back, smoothed his thumbs over her cheeks.

"No. I'm a jerk, Erin. You're right. None of this is your fault. It's easier to be angry at the school and you than to admit how badly Jenna has screwed things up. To admit that I stood by and let her."

"You didn't—"

"I should have known more about her new guy. Should have realized he was bad news and protected her and Rhett. Hell, the whole reason I moved to Colorado was to take care of things, and I let myself believe that just my mere presence here would make everything fine. I was a fool."

"You're here and you're trying. Give yourself a break."

He shook his head. "I can't. The stakes are too high."

She wanted to wipe the pain from his eyes, to take some of that burden and carry it for him. He'd uprooted his life to take care of his sister and nephew. He moved halfway across the country and had become a successful business owner and part of this town. There had never even been a question that he would step in for Rhett and get Jenna the help she needed. David was a good man, but he refused to see that in himself. Erin wished she could find a way to show him.

"I'd like to talk to Rhett." She forced herself to step out of David's embrace. It was too easy to forget that their relationship wasn't actually a relationship. He needed her help with his nephew, and she'd made the commitment to give it.

His attention wasn't about her—not really. She'd had a crush on him for far too long and he hadn't even known she existed. If it wasn't for the fact that she'd inserted herself into his life, he'd still be nothing more than her fantasy man and she'd be…nothing to him.

"We were watching a few minutes of television," he said, then glanced at his watch. "It's almost bedtime." He reached around her to shut the door to the staircase, then led her down the hall toward the main section of the apartment. They passed through the kitchen, which looked like a cozier version of the pub decor. The cabinets were dark wood with dark gray concrete countertops. Four chairs were tucked against the long island, exact copies of the bar stools downstairs.

"Dinner?" she asked, pointing to a half loaf of bread and jar of peanut butter sitting on the cluttered countertop.

David shrugged. "I tried to make grilled cheese sandwiches but burned the hell out of them. PB&J was the best I could do."

"Grilled cheese can be complicated," she said gently, earning a small laugh from David.

"It's better when I bring up food from downstairs," he admitted.

The far end of the kitchen opened to a family room, with wide-plank wood floors and oversize furniture. She could see *The Lego Movie* playing on the flat-screen TV that hung on one wall, and Rhett glanced up as they approached, then did a double take when he saw her.

"I got aspended," he announced, his voice solemn. "I can't come to school tomorrow."

"I know," she said, lowering herself to the cushion next to him. "That's why I stopped by tonight. I wanted to tell you that I'm sorry I wasn't at school today to help you on the playground."

"Uncle David said I can't hit people," Rhett told her, "even when they're mean."

"That's good advice." She reached out and gently smoothed away the hair that was falling across Rhett's eyes. "You can always talk to another teacher or Ms. Henderson if I'm not there."

"I hate Isaac." Rhett held his hands tight in his lap. "He called Mommy a bad word. It's not her fault his daddy wants to be her boyfriend. Lots of people want to be her boyfriend."

Erin heard a sound from David that sounded like a growl but focused her attention on the boy. "You love your mommy very much," she told him. "She's lucky to have you and I bet she's working hard to feel better and misses you so much."

"I miss her," Rhett whispered.

"I know you won't be at school tomorrow, but I hope your uncle will bring you to the community center in the afternoon. You can draw a picture for your mommy that shows how much you love her to give to her when she comes home."

Rhett looked from Erin to David. "Can I go, Uncle David?"

"Sure, buddy," came the rumbly response. "As long as you promise no more fights."

The boy nodded, then yawned. "I promise," he said sleepily.

"Time for bed," David announced.

"Can Ms. MacDonald read me a story?" Rhett asked, scooting off the couch.

David cleared his throat and Erin glanced back at him. He lifted one brow, silently leaving the decision up to her. Her life before last week had been so simple and straightforward. And boring.

"I'd love to," she told Rhett, and her heart melted a little when he grabbed her hand to lead her out of the family room.

She loved the hugs and hand-holding from her students, but there were always some who remained physically distant and she tried to respect that, too. Rhett had been one of those this year, which made the fact that he was reaching out to her mean so much more.

Glancing over her shoulder, she saw David watching them with an unreadable expression. Maybe she'd overstayed her welcome, but it felt right to be part of their lives.

"Are you okay if I check in downstairs for a minute?" he asked. "I'll be back up to tuck him in."

"Take your time." She handed him Tracie's keys and turned back to Rhett.

The boy led her down the hall to a small bedroom with a bathroom connected to it. It was clearly a guest room, with just a bed and nondescript chest of drawers against one wall. Rhett's stuffed blue dog sat on top of the plain beige comforter and there was a basket filled with random toys shoved in the corner.

Rhett grabbed the same pair of football-themed pajamas he'd been wearing the night of his mother's party from a pile of clothes stuffed into a laundry basket and spilling over onto the floor. "I need to get my pj's on and brush my teeth before we read."

"Is it okay if I fold some of your laundry while you do that?" she asked.

"I guess. Uncle David washes my clothes but says there's no point in putting anything away when I'm just going to wear them again."

Erin tried to keep her smile from showing. That was exactly something a single man would say. "Is that what you did with your mommy?"

Rhett shook his head. "Mommy and me folded laundry after dinner. I did the socks."

"Then I'll save the socks for you," Erin said.

"I'm good at them," Rhett confirmed, and disappeared into the bathroom.

She heard the sound of water running and then Rhett brushing his teeth. She folded the clothes and put them away in drawers, hoping that small thing would help him feel more settled.

It made her feel like she was contributing something, making up for how she hadn't been there for him earlier. Rationally she knew it wasn't her fault. Her work on the district planning committee had taken her out of the building for a day of training. Teachers got subs all the time for a variety of reasons. But it didn't change the fact that the boy had needed her, and she'd failed him.

She couldn't let it happen again.

After a few minutes, Rhett returned to the bedroom.

"Dirty clothes in the laundry hamper," she said, pointing to a wicker basket next to the dresser.

"You sound like Mommy," he told her as he went back to retrieve his discarded clothes. But he was smiling as he climbed on the bed next to her. The first smile she'd seen from him tonight.

He rolled the socks into balls, then handed her a Magic Tree House book from the nightstand. She made sure he was snuggled in tight, then started to read about ninjas and two time-traveling kids.

She finished a chapter, then glanced down at Rhett to see his eyes had drifted shut, Ruffie tucked under his arm. She stood slowly and smoothed the covers over both the boy and the stuffed dog. Erin had so much in her life—a great job, good friends, a mom who loved her. But there was nothing she could truly call her own, and spending time with Rhett made it clear how much she wanted that.

The relentless pounding in her chest sounded strangely like her ovaries stomping their tiny reproductive feet, as if to say, "it's about time you remembered we were withering away here." Well, not exactly withering. She had plenty of time to settle down. The scary truth was that she was already settled but seemed destined to be stuck alone.

She wanted to change her life, but maybe it had been a mistake to focus on her professional life when her personal world was so sorely lacking any excitement. David McCay would be an adventure—the kind that could ruin her for any other man. It might just be worth the risk. She shook her head and commanded her ovaries to shut down the party. This was the kind of thinking that had led to her outrageous request, and she didn't need to revisit that moment.

After returning the book to the nightstand, she turned to find David watching her from the doorway. Color rushed to her cheeks as if he could read her thoughts.

He stepped back just enough to let her out, then moved forward to place a gentle kiss on Rhett's forehead and tuck the sheets around him.

When Rhett was settled, David pulled the door shut and motioned her down the hall. "Did I hear you tell your ovaries to shut up?" he asked when they reached the kitchen.

She clasped a hand over her mouth to stifle a hysterical giggle. "Of course not," she said in a rush of air. "That would be crazy. Do I seem crazy to you?"

"At this point," he said after studying her for several moments, "you seem like a gift from heaven."

Oh. Well, that was unexpected. And lovely.

"I'm doing my job," she answered automatically.

"How does finagling the key to my apartment from Tracie fall under a teacher's job description?"

"I wanted to check on Rhett."

He moved closer, crowding her a little. But she didn't step back even though that was her inclination. She stood her ground. "That's not all you want," he whispered.

There weren't enough words in the English language to cover all the things she wanted from David. From life. From this moment.

"Ask me again," he told her, threading his fingers through her hair. The desire she saw in his blue eyes mesmerized her. A longing that matched her own, making her need grow that much more intense. "Ask me to have an affair with you."

"Kiss me," she said instead. Those two words were the only ones she could force her mouth to form at the moment.

He lowered his mouth to hers, claiming her lips with a force she felt all the way to her toes. How could the way he touched her feel both infinitely gentle and demanding at the same time? She wound her arms around his neck and gave herself over to the sensation. It was too much and not enough, and she whispered the one word that pounded through her whole body. "More."

Chapter Seven

It was like the Fourth of July inside David's brain. He'd kissed plenty of women—taken some of them to his bed—girlfriends and baseball groupies who made it their mission to snag a professional athlete. None of them had affected him the way Erin did.

He wanted to blame it on his basically celibate lifestyle since settling in Crimson, but he knew it was more than that. It was the woman in his arms.

A shiver passed through her when he sucked her sensitive earlobe into his mouth. He lifted her onto the edge of the counter and positioned himself against the sweet V of her body, even as he did his best to keep his raging lust under control.

She deserved more than he could ever offer her in life, but the least he could do was refrain from mauling her like some sort of randy teenager. He wanted to savor each moment they spent together, to get down on his knees and worship every inch of her—to beg her to stay with him.

His hands trembled as he undid the buttons of her crisp linen blouse, revealing a pale blue bra covering the most beautiful breasts he'd ever seen. His mouth went dry and all he could do was stare at the creamy skin, flushed with pink.

He traced one finger over the edge of the fabric, earning a whispered moan from Erin.

"Amazing," he murmured, and she shook her head.

"You don't have to say that. My body is average at best." He'd heard plenty of women disparage themselves, mostly fishing for more compliments, but Erin made the statement like it was a well-known fact.

"Nothing about you is average."

She flashed a self-deprecating smile. "Everything about me is average."

"No." He placed a finger to her lips when she would have argued. "You have a gorgeous face and the most kissable skin." He trailed his mouth down the long column of her throat, and it almost drove him over the edge when she dropped back onto her elbows, pressing her breasts high into the air.

"The best part is that the way you look is only part of what makes you beautiful. When we're together, I feel things I didn't know were a possibility for a guy like me." He swirled his tongue around the tip of her breast through the fabric of her bra.

She moaned and he gathered her close, kissing her with all of his pent-up desire, letting her feel exactly how much he wanted her. She tugged on his T-shirt and he pulled it over his head and let it drop to the floor. Her hands smoothed up his chest, making his breath catch. His whole body pounded with need.

He wanted to strip off her clothes and feast on her.

He wanted to lose himself in the moment and take her, make her his.

No.

A woman like Erin would never be his. Reality came crashing down around him, and he jerked back.

She stared at him, her gaze hazy with lust. Her breasts rose and fell as she struggled to make her breathing normal again. She sat on the edge of his counter, soft and sexy and ready for him. Hell, she had no idea how sexy she was.

"I'm sorry," he said, and wanted to punch his own face as her gaze clouded with doubt and then embarrassment.

She scrambled off the counter and turned away, quickly buttoning up her blouse. "Do I thank you now?" she asked quietly, the ice in her tone cutting across his skin. "Are we even? I came to see Rhett and you gave me a little taste—" she waved her hand toward the counter "—of that. I should be grateful, right?"

"Don't say that." He spun her around to face him. "Don't make this into something it isn't."

"I have a pretty good idea of exactly what this is and isn't," she said, her tone miserable.

"You have no idea." He ran a hand through his hair, trying to figure out how kissing this woman had become so complicated. Sex had always been simple. Straightforward. Meaningless. The fact that he wanted it to be so much more with Erin scared the hell out of him.

But the last thing he wanted was for her to believe he didn't want her.

"You mean something," he said. "To Rhett." He cleared his throat. "To me."

She bit down on her lip and he had to stifle a groan.

"I'm his teacher," she said without emotion. "I'm helping you manage these weeks without your sister."

"It's more than that," he said. "I like you, Erin."

"Enough to kiss me," she said through clenched teeth, "but not enough for sex."

"That isn't what this is about. You're not the kind of woman I want to sleep with—"

"I get it," she said, blinking rapidly.

Damn. He hoped like hell she wasn't going to cry. He was making a total mess of everything.

"We're obviously done here." She offered him a stiff little wave. "I assume it's okay if I let myself out the front door?"

He wrapped his fingers around her wrist and pulled her close. "I'm trying to give you a compliment. You deserve more than a quick roll in the sheets after an exhausting day. You're the kind of woman who men take on dates and home to meet their parents. I told you, you're apple pie and white picket fences. I'm late nights wrangling drunk tourists at a bar."

She tugged her wrist out of his grasp. "You're a baseball player," she said, spitting out the words like an accusation.

"Not anymore."

That earned him an eye roll. "You were a famous pitcher for a major-league team. Talk about the American ideal. It's our national pastime."

"I'm not good for you."

She threw up her hands. "Why does everyone think they know what I want more clearly than I do? My mom thinks my expectations of life are too high. My ex thinks I can't be adventurous in the bedroom because I don't have the body of a stripper. You want me up on some holier-than-thou pedestal."

"Your body is perfect," he said, wishing he could punch whatever idiot boyfriend had made her believe otherwise.

"Yeah," she said on a derisive laugh. "Really hard for you to resist. But someone in this town is going to want me." Her voice cracked a tiny bit and she sucked in a breath. "Even for one night. Hey, we're standing above a bar. I bet I can find a guy downstairs willing to be with me."

She turned on her heel and stalked toward the door to his loft. "Bring Rhett to the community center tomorrow at four," she called over her shoulder.

As angry as she was with David, she was still looking after Rhett. Taking care of both of them, really. And David was watching her walk away to find another man.

How big of an idiot could he be?

He caught up to her just as she reached for the door handle.

"Go on a date with me," he said, pressing his hand to the door to keep it shut.

She stilled, but it took her a minute to lift her gaze to his. "What?"

"We can go to dinner or on a hike or whatever you want."

Her eyes narrowed. "Why are you asking me out? Is this more payback for helping with Rhett? I care about him. You don't have to—"

He brushed his lips across hers. "Do you always argue when a man asks you on a date?" he asked against her mouth, then leaned in to press his forehead to hers, the tips of their noses touching.

She inhaled, her warm breath tickling his skin. "I'm not your type," she said.

"No," he countered. "I'm not *your* type. You deserve way better than me. But I'm asking anyway. Go out with me."

She didn't answer for so long he thought she might decline the invitation. He didn't blame her. He knew what he had to offer someone like her. A whole lot of drama and baggage. It would have been smarter to have just taken what she offered earlier. Maybe he could have gotten her out of his system.

But he wanted more.

"Okay," she said when he started to pull back.

He grinned, feeling like he'd just purchased a winning lottery ticket. "I'll call you," he said.

"Really?" She laughed softly. "We could just grab dinner after you pick up Rhett tomorrow night."

"Nope. I'm going to call you, and we'll make a plan and it will be like…"

"A date?"

"Like we're courting," he answered, the sound and connotation of the old-fashioned word appealing to him. Thanks to the baseball groupies who had hung around the fields since high school, David had never had to try hard with women. They fell into his lap—sometimes literally.

The idea of actually making an effort was new and strangely exciting. The thought of earning his place at Erin's side made nerves flutter through his chest.

"Courting," she repeated. "Are you sure?"

"Absolutely," he said, and kissed her again.

Then he opened the door. "I'll talk to you soon."

She looked slightly puzzled, which he found adorable. He wanted to keep her guessing.

She'd just started down the stairs when he called her name.

"Um…" He ran a hand through his hair, uncharacteristically anxious. "I hope this means you aren't heading downstairs to look for a guy. I know you don't owe me anything but—"

"I'm going home. Good night, David."

He blew out a breath as he closed the door. What the hell was he so nervous about? And possessive? He'd never cared before about being exclusive with the women he dated.

But it made him ridiculously happy to consider the possibility of Erin becoming his. He rubbed his shoulder as he moved through the apartment, turning off lights. It was still early compared to his normal hours, but David was tired as hell. All he wanted was to drop into his bed and dream of Erin.

Rhett tugged on Erin's arm as she handed Mari Clayton, the program director for the Aspen Foundation, her grant paperwork the following afternoon. It was just after six, and the other kids who'd come for tutoring and after-school activities had been picked up already. David was running a few minutes late so Rhett had been playing with Lego blocks while Erin began the meeting with the woman she hoped would fund Crimson Kidzone so it could be expanded. Erin needed the money to hire a part-time staff person.

There was so much she wanted to do for kids in the Crimson community now that she'd started, but all of it took money. Mari seemed receptive to her ideas, so Erin had high hopes that the grant request she was submitting would be approved.

"Excuse me for a moment," she said to Mari, and turned to Rhett. "What do you need, Rhett?"

"Isaac is here." The boy gave her a pained look. "And Mommy's boyfriend."

She turned to where he was pointing. Another boy with dark hair and eyes stood in the doorway to the community center's makeshift classroom.

She recognized Isaac Martin, the boy Rhett had fought with at school, although his family had moved to Crimson last year so she'd never had him in class.

He wore baggy sweatpants and a Denver Broncos jersey. Next to him stood a tall, lean man close to Erin's age whom she recognized as Joel Martin, Jenna McCay's boyfriend and Isaac's father. His black hair was slicked back from his face and, although his features were classically handsome, his eyes had a hard edge to them.

He met her gaze and gave her a quick once-over. Goose bumps shivered across her skin, and not the kind she got when David looked at her. This man's stare made her feel uncomfortable and strangely nervous. She saw his gaze switch to Mari for a second before dismissing her just as quickly as he had Erin.

"The lady at the desk said this is where I sign my kid up for day care," the man said, arms crossed over his chest.

Isaac glared at Rhett, who moved behind Erin's legs, holding tight to the denim of the dark-washed jeans she wore.

"I'd be happy to get you an enrollment form," she answered. "Although it's not exactly day care." She threw Mari an apologetic glance. "I offer an after-school enrichment program three days a week and—"

"Whatever," the man said. "Can I leave him now? His mom don't get off work until seven and I have things to do. His sisters are with their dad tonight and he don't want to stay by himself."

Erin had spoken to Melody after the fight about Isaac's family situation. According to her friend, the boy had two older stepsisters but his mother was single and struggling to keep her household together.

"Isaac is welcome to be part of the program," she said, keeping her voice steady, "but it only goes until six and he can't start until the paperwork is completed."

"*He's* still here." The man pointed at Rhett. "Isaac and him can play."

Rhett dug his fingers into her legs, and she wanted to wrap him in her arms. Isaac glared at them both. His father shifted to get a better look at Rhett, then did a double take.

"That's Jenna's kid," he muttered, then swatted Isaac on the back of the head. "He's the one that hit you, right?"

"Mr. Martin, what happened between the boys is a matter for the school to deal with. Rhett is going to be picked up in a few minutes, and I can get you an enrollment form but—"

"How's your mama doing, boy? It was a shame the crap got out of hand that night. I'm looking forward to her getting back so—"

Suddenly Joel jerked back as David spun him around and slammed him against the wall, pressing his forearm to the other man's throat. "You won't see my sister again. You won't look at her. You won't acknowledge her existence. Are we clear?"

Mari Clayton gasped and Erin peeled Rhett's hands off her legs and hurried forward. What kind of example were these two grown men showing boys who had just been disciplined for fighting? Not to mention the fact that the last thing Erin needed was a scene in the middle of her meeting with a potential donor.

Joel coughed and fought, but David had at least thirty pounds on him and showed no sign of backing down.

"Get the hell off me," Joel bit out, his voice hoarse. "Jenna can make her own damn decisions."

"Tell me you're going to leave my sister alone."

Erin didn't recognize this version of David. Gone was the laid-back bar owner or the caring—if sometimes clueless—uncle. Anger and violence radiated from him, making him seem like the man he'd warned her about.

Isaac had moved back into the hall, his small body shrinking against the door frame.

"David." She placed a hand on his arm. "Stop. This isn't the place. You're scaring the boys."

"Listen to the lady," Joel said, but as soon as David loosened his grip, the other man struck out, his fist connecting with David's jaw.

Erin heard a scream and realized it came from her throat. David shoved Joel again, and the tall man stumbled into the wall.

"Enough," she shouted.

Both men stilled at her tone. She might be shaking with nerves, but she had enough experience as a teacher to take command of the situation.

"The community center," she said slowly, as if settling a dispute over a favorite crayon, "is not the place for you two to have this..." She searched for the right word and settled on "conversation. You both have boys watching your every move."

David pressed a hand to his jaw and glanced over his shoulder to where Rhett was staring, wide-eyed, at the scene playing out in front of him.

"Dude grabbed me," Joel muttered. "I got to defend myself."

"Mr. Martin," she said firmly, "you can request a Kidzone enrollment form at the community center's front desk." She turned to Isaac and gentled her voice. "We'd love to have you in the program, but there is no fighting or name-calling here. It's a safe place for everyone. Do you understand?"

The boy's brows lowered but he nodded. His father muttered under his breath a string of expletives so explicit it made her breath catch in her throat. David moved forward again with a growl, and she stepped between the two men.

"It would be a good idea for you to leave now," she told Joel. "Isaac, I hope to see you next week."

Joel's upper lip curled into an ugly sneer as he narrowed his gaze on David. "A real man don't let no woman push him around. Your sister knows what it's like to be with a baller." His mean brown eyes shifted to Erin. "Maybe Ms. Teacher wants something more in her life, too. What you say, baby?"

David snarled and tried pushing around Erin. "I'm going to—"

"No." She took a step to the side so she was still blocking him. "Mr. Martin, you need to go."

With a sickeningly sweet smile and a salute, the man turned away. "Come on, Isaac. Let's blow this place."

Erin stood watching them walk down the hall for several moments, willing her breathing back to a normal pace.

"Erin." David's voice was gentle, but when he went to place a hand on her shoulder, she swatted away his touch.

"I'll deal with you in a minute," she said through teeth clenched tightly so no one would notice how much they were chattering. "Take care of Rhett. I have a meeting to finish."

Nervous laughter sounded from behind her. "I think we're finished here for tonight."

Mari Clayton had gathered her bag and purse and was staring at Erin and David, her cheeks flushed and a hand pressed flat to her chest.

"Uncle David," Rhett called. "You got in a fight just like me."

She heard David sigh as he moved toward his nephew. "I'm sorry about that," he said to Mari. "There was some history there but this wasn't the time or place for us to play it out."

The woman swallowed and nodded. "I understand."

He turned back to Erin, but she gave him a quelling glare, then focused her attention on Mari. "You can't possibly understand."

"You're right. This felt more like *Fight Club* than an after-school program for kids. I applaud what you're trying to do, Erin, and it's clear the community needs a safe place for kids to go. Still, I'm not sure your program and the Aspen Foundation are a good fit."

Tears stung the back of Erin's eyes. It was adrenaline, she knew, but this was not how the meeting with Mari was supposed to end. "I apologize for the scene. But I hope you'll change your mind. I think this demonstrates just how important a community outreach program that brings kids together is for Crimson."

"But can you keep the children safe?"

There was a slight hint of accusation in Mari's tone; Erin's doubts crashed around her like a thousand ocean waves. Her mother's refrain of "be happy with good enough" rang through her mind. Kidzone had been in place one week and already there was a question about whether she could manage it.

"I firmly believe I can," she lied to her potential donor. She wanted to make a safe place for kids to come after school, but Erin knew better than most that wanting something and getting it weren't always the same thing.

"Let's touch base in a few weeks," Mari said noncommittally. "The decisions about our fall funding cycle will be made by the end of October. It may be better to wait until your program is more established."

Biting down on the inside of her cheek to keep from crying, Erin nodded. A moment after Mari walked away, Olivia appeared in the doorway. "Is everything all right? Rita said a guy just stormed by the front desk, dragging a boy along with him."

"A potential client," Erin said, shaking her head.

"Isaac's daddy is mean," Rhett whispered.

"No way are you going to let that kid in here."

She turned from Olivia to see David staring at her, hands on hips, his features hard as granite.

Olivia stepped forward. "Rhett, I was about to box up the cupcakes someone brought in today. Would you help me, and you can take a couple home for you and your uncle?"

"It's fine, buddy," David said when the boy looked up at him. "Ms. MacDonald and I will work things out in here."

Rhett moved toward Olivia.

"I'm going to ask Mommy," he told Erin as he passed, "not to be his girlfriend anymore when she gets back."

"I'm sorry he scared you," she said, reaching out to ruffle his hair. "You know you're always safe with me."

He nodded. "Can I bring a cupcake for Ms. MacDonald, too?" he asked Olivia.

"You bet," she answered and took his hand to lead him away.

As soon as the boy was gone, all of the adrenaline that had kept Erin together through that ugly scene drained from her body. She dropped her head into her hands and drew in a deep breath.

"Erin."

She glanced up to see David taking a step closer. "Don't," she whispered, and automatically moved back. "You don't get to tell me how to run this program. You certainly don't get to make a scene in front of the foundation representative I was hoping would give me the money to hire additional staff and really make this thing work."

"I didn't realize who she was," he said, rubbing a hand over the shadow of stubble across his jaw.

She hated that even now, as angry as she was with

him, the scratchy sound still made her tingle all the way to her toes.

"It doesn't matter," she said, crossing her arms over her chest. "You were out of line."

His head snapped back as if she'd struck him. "You heard what he was saying about Jenna. The things he insinuated toward you. I'm not going to stand by and let a creep like that get away with—"

"You're Rhett's guardian now, David. His role model. How can you expect him to work out his problems without violence when you set that kind of example?" She knew she was being harsh, but her emotions wouldn't let her back down. "Joel Martin is awful but there are better ways to deal with him."

"What ways?" he countered. "Watching the guy get away with whatever he wants? Letting his kid bully my nephew and disrespect you and my sister?"

"I don't need you to protect me."

He barked out a laugh. "It sounds like you don't need me at all."

She bit down on her lip, unsure of how to respond. She didn't want to need him but couldn't resist the current of awareness pulsing between them, despite their differences and her anger.

"Thank you for keeping Rhett today," he said quietly, smoothing a finger over the furrow she knew formed between her brows when she was upset. "I'm sorry I screwed things up with your meeting. I wasn't joking when I told you I was bad news, Erin. This afternoon proves my point."

"David."

He dropped his finger to her lip. "You've gone out of your way to help me, and I'm grateful. What happened here was a crappy way to show it."

Before she could respond, he dropped his hand and walked out of the room, presumably to collect Rhett from Olivia.

Erin wanted to rush after him, to launch herself at his big frame and hold on tight. David didn't belong to her, but her chest ached at the thought of losing him. She'd managed to carve out a decent life for herself, and she should be satisfied with that. It was easier and a lot less pain in the long run.

Chapter Eight

When the doorbell rang that night, David's heart leaped. He rubbed at his chest as he went to answer it, hope rising like a bird on a current of air that Erin was paying him a visit.

He hated himself for hurting her, then walking away. He'd sat on the couch since putting Rhett to bed with his phone in his hand, typing out a half dozen texts but deleting each one.

She'd seen his true colors, although it might be better that it happened now instead of down the road. If he'd actually had the opportunity to truly claim her as his own, he wasn't sure he'd ever be able to let her go.

But hope was a painfully resilient emotion, unwilling to let go of even the briefest glimpse of happiness. If Erin had come to him, maybe he still had a chance. With a deep breath, he opened the door.

"Hello, David. It's been a while."

Without his hand gripping the door handle, David would have stumbled back a step. His mouth went dry and it felt like someone had dropped a lead balloon on his chest. "Mom."

"Are you going to invite me in?" Angela McCay peered around him into the apartment. "Kind of a fancy place you've set yourself up in, even if you're living over a bar."

"Mom, why are you here?"

She smoothed a hand over her hair and flashed him a sad smile. "Isn't it obvious? I'm making things right."

He hadn't seen his mother in over five years, but she looked the same as ever. It was as if Angela drank from the fountain of youth and never aged. Her blond hair was shorter than he remembered, a simple cut that fell to just above her shoulders. Maybe there were a few thin lines etched into the skin around her vivid blue eyes.

But she remained as beautiful as she'd been when he was a boy. At Rhett's age, David would sit on one of the chairs in the kitchen and watch her move about the room—on the rare occasions when she cooked a real dinner—and think how lucky he was to have Angela as his mother. It took him a while to learn that a person's outward beauty wasn't always an accurate measure of who they were on the inside.

Too much had happened in their small family, terrible things and small mistreatments that his mother had either been responsible for or turned a blind eye to as they unfolded. He wished he could recapture some of his unconditional love from childhood, but he was an adult and had spent too long nursing old wounds to let them go so easily.

Yet she was still his mother, so he stepped back to let her into his apartment and, he supposed, his life.

"Did Jenna call you?"

"Yes, and it's about time," his mom answered as she

moved past him. “My bags are in the hall. Be a good boy and bring them in for me.”

“Bags?” he asked even as he pulled in the two suitcases and closed the door. “How long do you plan to be here?”

She turned to him. “As long as it takes. Your sister wants me here. She thinks you need help.”

“I’m not the one in rehab,” he muttered.

“That might have been a bit of overkill,” she said, arching one brow. “Jenna could have recovered on her own.”

“We’ve tried that before. It didn’t take, and Rhett is old enough now to be affected. She needs to get healthy, and it has to stick this time.”

She studied him for a moment, then sighed. “You always were her knight in shining armor.” She stepped closer and raised a hand to his cheek. “You took care of both of us.”

The scent of her shampoo, honey and almond, drifted up to him, taking him back to sharing a bathroom in their tiny apartment growing up. He’d taken countless lukewarm showers as a kid after his mom and sister used up their limited supply of hot water, but he’d always loved the way the bathroom smelled after his mother got ready.

“I did a sucky job at it,” he said, letting his eyes drift closed and losing himself in the familiar touch and scent.

She patted his cheek. “You tried, and that’s what counts.”

If someone had asked, David would have claimed he didn’t need anything from his mother. Not her help, not her approval and certainly not her blessing. Yet those words of absolution seemed to loosen the chains that were locked tight around his heart. They didn’t eliminate his guilt and regret, but somehow they made him feel better.

“You tried, too,” he told her, his way of offering an olive branch after so many years of animosity between them.

"We both know I didn't," she said quietly. "I was a hot mess, and you and your sister got pulled into it. I thought baseball was your ticket out until the accident..."

"It wasn't an accident." He took a step away and crossed his arms over his chest. "It was a stupid bar fight, and I never should have been there in the first place."

She gave him a speculative look. "And now you own a bar."

"It's a brewpub, Mom. I'm good at making beer." He laughed softly. "Maybe better than I was at pitching."

"How's your shoulder?"

"Fine."

"Do you ever think about going back?"

A familiar tension pulsed through his body, making his blood feel like it was tinged with acid. He'd spent months rehabbing his shoulder with grueling exercise and physical therapy. He refused to believe that stupidity had ended his baseball career in a matter of minutes. Guys came back from injuries and surgeries—sometimes better than they'd been in the first place.

Not David.

He paced to the edge of the living room, glancing out at the view of Main Street from his front window. If it weren't for Jenna's move to Colorado and his frustration over a shoulder that wouldn't return to its normal strength, this town would mean nothing to him. But Crimson had been the best thing to happen to him. It made the ache of losing baseball—his escape and sanctuary—tolerable. Even from his place on the periphery, this community had helped him to stop looking back to what could have been and focus on the life he had.

"Not anymore," he told his mother. "My life is good now. Healthy. I want that for Rhett and Jenna." He moved toward her. "I need help, and if you're willing to give it you can stay. But we're doing things my way. There are rules and structure."

Angela made a face. "I've never been much for structure, honey. You know that. I'm here to bring some fun and sunshine into that boy's life."

Which sounded like his mother blowing sunshine. But if Jenna had called her, he would make it work. "Fun is fine," he said, resisting the urge to roll his eyes. "But he needs a routine. We're giving him that, and we're going to do the same for Jenna when she gets back. She's got to clean up her life, whether she likes it or not."

His mother rose to her tiptoes and kissed his cheek. "Your sister is lucky to have you. It's not too late for our family, David."

He hoped she was right. "You can stay in my bedroom. I'll take the couch."

"I don't want to be an imposition," his mother said, even as she shrugged out of her brightly colored cardigan and draped it over the back of the couch. "Will you be a dear and bring my bags? Do I have my own bathroom?"

Before David could answer, a small voice called his name. "Uncle David?"

He turned see Rhett standing at the edge of the hallway, wiping the back of his hand across his eyes.

"Is Mommy here? I woke up and heard her voice."

David heard a tiny gasp behind him. He was used to how much Jenna and their mother looked alike but hadn't realized they sounded similar, as well.

"Your mom isn't here," he said gently. "But your grandma has come to visit." He moved to reveal Angela standing behind him.

"Hi, sweetie boy," she cooed. "Do you remember your grandma?"

Rhett shook his head.

Angela made a sound of distress, then pasted a bright smile on her face. "You were a baby the last time I saw you. It was before you and your mommy moved to Colorado." She stepped forward. "I'm going to help Uncle David look after you until she comes home, okay? We're going to have lots of fun together."

Rhett slanted his head, studying Angela. "You don't look like a grandma," he said.

David gave a small snort of laughter, earning a narrow-eyed glare from his mother. She reached for the sweater and quickly put it on over the silky tank top she wore underneath. Angela had never dressed like a typical mother, either.

"Doesn't change the fact that I'm yours," she said. "You good with that?"

Rhett's sleepy blue gaze met David's. "Your mom called your grandmother," David told the boy. "So she could stay with us."

After a moment Rhett nodded. "Okay."

"Time to go back to bed," David told the boy.

"I can tuck you in," Angela offered.

"I want Uncle David," Rhett whispered.

David felt his heart clutch, but heard his mother sigh. "You bet, buddy." He put a hand on his mother's shoulder. Although he'd never had much sympathy for her, he understood what it was like to be unsure how to do what was right.

"Give it time," he whispered, and took Rhett's hand.

He led the boy back to his bedroom, retrieved Ruffie from the far side of the bed and settled Rhett under the covers again.

By the time he came out, his mother had moved her bags into his bedroom. She'd taken his clothes out of the dresser and filled a laundry basket.

"I hope you don't mind if I unpack," she said, folding a stack of more tank tops. "I hate living out of a suitcase."

He thought about asking her about her current life and if she had a home base now. Other than a monthly bank transfer into her checking account, David wasn't exactly up to date on his mother's life. But he could save that for another night. Apparently, they'd have plenty if she was here until Jenna returned.

"Rhett doesn't normally wake during the night," he told her. "Since you're here, I'm going to go downstairs and check on the bar."

She raised one finely penciled eyebrow. "Are *you* drinking, David?"

"Mom, I brew beer for a living. I drink, but it's not a problem."

She tsked softly.

He sighed. "I haven't been drunk since the night of the bar fight."

"At least I would have understood if you'd been drinking when you gave that woman and her boyfriend most of your money. I'm not so sure about your decision-making when you're sober."

"I put that man in the hospital for almost a month. Everything changed in one moment. I owed them."

"He fell and knocked his head on the corner of the table."

"Because I punched him."

"After he knifed you."

"I'm not having this discussion again," he said through gritted teeth. "Jenna wants you here, and I'll honor that. But I'm not rehashing old history. I don't get drunk anymore, and I watch my temper. Things are good in Crimson, and I intend to keep it that way."

She studied him a long moment, then nodded. "Fine.

Go do what you need to do. I'll be here if my grandson needs me."

David nodded and headed for Elevation. Halfway down his private staircase, he stopped. His chest rose and fell and it felt like someone had lobbed a grenade at him. How the hell had his life spun so out of control? He was the temporary guardian for his five-year-old nephew and his mother—who had the maternal instincts of a feral cat—was now his child-rearing partner?

He turned and took the steps back to his apartment two at a time. Grabbing his jacket and the set of keys off the hook on the wall, he let himself out the front door and walked toward his truck parked in the alley behind the building.

He had plenty to take care of at both the bar and the brewery, but there was other business that called to him in his current mood.

Erin looked out the peephole of her apartment's front door and sucked in a breath.

"I know you're in there," David said softly, sounding like a man who had the patience to wait all night for her if that's how she played it. "Talk to me, Erin. Please."

Damn her weakness for good manners. A well-timed "please" got her every time.

She opened the door a few inches and tried not to notice how gorgeous he looked standing on the other side. He wore dark jeans, engineer boots and a heavy canvas jacket to ward against the crisp evening temperatures that signaled fall in the mountains. His hair was disheveled, like the wind was blowing or he'd been running his hands through it.

The way she wanted to run her hands through it.

"Can I come in?" he asked in that same quiet tone that made his already low voice sound like a growl.

"Where's Rhett?"

"Asleep," he answered automatically. "My mom is at the apartment in case he wakes up."

"You have a mom?" Erin was so shocked she stepped back and the door opened a little wider.

One side of David's mouth quirked up. "Would you like to see my belly button to prove I'm not an alien?"

Her mouth went dry as she glanced at the edge of his jacket. *Heck, yes*, her body screamed. *Take off your clothes, hottie brewmaster.*

"No," she said, her voice coming out a chirp. "I know you're human, but I didn't realize your mom was coming to visit."

She wanted to smack herself on the head. Of course she didn't know anything about his mother. The intimacy between her and David had developed too quickly and under such strange circumstances.

"If you invite me in, I'll tell you about it." He leaned closer. "Your neighbor's front curtains are fluttering like mad. I swear she's going to call the cops, and the last thing I need is Cole coming after me."

"That's Ms. Kronkowski," Erin said without even having to look at which apartment he was talking about. "Because I'm single she thinks I must be a wild party girl."

David chuckled.

"Hey," she said, pushing at his chest. "That's not funny."

"Yes, it is." His eyes grazed up and down her body and she realized she'd let the door open enough that her Hello Kitty pajamas were on full display. "It's not even ten and you're ready for bed."

"I was reading," she countered.

"Let me guess," he said. "A romance novel."

She narrowed her eyes, not sure how she felt about him pegging her reading tastes so easily. "What do you have against heroes?"

"I don't trust 'em," he said with a shrug. "If a guy seems too good to be true, he probably is."

"Not on my e-reader," she answered, but gestured him into the apartment, both because she didn't want Ms. Kronkowski to go apoplectic and because Erin's ex-boyfriend had seemed too good to be true. And he'd turned out to be a first-class jerk.

"Tell me about the guy who hurt you," David said, pulling the door shut and coming to stand in front of her.

Could he read her mind? She gave a strangled laugh and asked, "Is that why you're here?"

He shook his head. "I'm here to apologize, but I want to know about you."

"There's nothing to know. If you don't believe me, talk to my mother. She'll be happy to tell you how ordinary I am."

When his gaze turned sympathetic, Erin closed her eyes and sighed. "I didn't mean that. I don't want to talk about my ex-boyfriend or my mother with you."

He laced his fingers with hers when she opened her eyes, then led her to the couch, taking a seat and tugging her down next to him.

"I'll start," he told her, using his thumb to trace circles around the center of her palm. The featherlight touch made her skin tingle. "I'm sorry I lost it today at the community center. I was out of line, and the last thing I want to do is jeopardize your program. You've been a lifesaver for me, and you deserve better in return."

"Every kid gets a chance," she told him, "even the ones

with awful parents. I can't turn away a child because you have a personal issue with his father."

"I get that," he said, "even if I don't like it. Hell, maybe if Jenna and I had a teacher like you back in the day, things could have been different for us." He dropped his head to the back of the couch, staring up at the white ceiling in her apartment. "Which brings me to my mother. She showed up tonight because my sister called her to help. She seems sincere, but things have never been great with us. Motherhood wasn't really her thing, so Jenna and I did a lot of raising ourselves."

"You took care of your sister," Erin said quietly.

"Not very well," he told her, pulling his hand away. "I was obsessed with playing baseball. The funny thing was that one of Mom's boyfriends actually bought me my first ball and bat. He was a third baseman in the minor leagues, a decent guy." He gave a half-hearted chuckle. "Of course, that meant he and my mom didn't last long. She was a magnet for losers, just like Jenna. But I kept playing ball."

"And you were good," she said. "I Googled you."

"You Googled me," he repeated softly. "I can't even imagine the crap you found about me online."

She shrugged. "You've had an exciting life."

"Hardly." He shook his head. "I screwed the whole thing up."

"Because of your injury," she prompted.

"I don't talk about it."

"You can with me."

He studied her a moment, then nodded. "It was a stupid bar fight. I'd met a woman after one of our home games and we started hooking up. It wasn't love or dating. I didn't know anything about her other than she was hot. I was twenty-five and stupid as the day is long. I had an ego to match my pitching talent. The woman had a jealous husband."

"She was married?"

He gave a sharp nod. "I swear I didn't know that, but it doesn't matter. We were out and her husband came busting into the bar, hell-bent on beating me to a pulp. He was a big guy."

"You're a big guy."

"I was also drunk and sloppy. But I'm a decent fighter. Just not against a knife."

"David," she whispered, noticing that he'd moved his hand to massage his shoulder.

"In retrospect," he said quietly, "that guy did me a favor."

"He ended your career."

"My reckless behavior ended it, and who knows where I'd be if it hadn't happened. I wouldn't have moved to Crimson to help Jenna." He gave her a lopsided smile. "I wouldn't have met you."

"Oh," she breathed, because somewhere in his words was the nicest compliment she'd ever received.

"From my perspective, ordinary is the most exciting thing going." He draped an arm across the couch cushions, his fingers just grazing her back. The gentle touch made her body come alive.

"There's nothing exciting about my life," she said, shaking her head.

"Come on," he prompted. "Give me more than that. Help me understand you, Erin. I know you're a great teacher, but I also know the program at the community center means more to you than just another way to help kids."

She bit down on her bottom lip, then sucked in a breath when he ran the pad of his thumb over the same spot.

"I want something that belongs to me," she said after a moment. "I want to do something that my mom can be proud of—"

"She should be proud that her daughter is one of the best teachers around."

If only it were that simple. "We moved to Crimson after my dad died when I was just a little older than Rhett. They were older when I was born." She cleared her throat and added, "I was definitely a surprise. Dad was a college professor and my mom is a psychiatrist. It was clear from the time I was little that I wasn't like them. They loved me, but I didn't quite fit. They were both so smart."

"You're smart."

"My mom is a legitimate genius and I'm—" she shrugged "—average."

"Don't say that."

"It's true. I wasn't the kid she expected to get. After Dad died, I'm not sure she knew what to do with me. I wanted to do things like Girl Scouts and slumber parties, and she thought I should be spending more time with my head in the books. When it became clear I wasn't going to live up to her high standards, she kind of lost interest."

"How could anyone lose interest in you?" He shifted closer, cupped her cheeks in his warm palms. "You're smart and beautiful, and you have the biggest heart of anyone I know."

"Apparently," she muttered, "big hearts aren't as valuable as big breasts."

He blinked and dropped his hands. "Come again."

"Have you heard of Brazen Peaks?"

"The restaurant outside of Carbondale?"

"I think the correct term is 'breastaurant,'" she told him.

"Right. So what?"

"Have you been there?"

He shook his head. "Not my scene."

"My ex met his new girlfriend there. According to him, she's sexy, adventurous and exciting." She made a face. "I'm pretty sure that means I'm none of those things."

"Or it means your ex is an idiot." He leaned and brushed his lips across hers. "Trust me. Your ex is an idiot."

She couldn't stop the smile that tugged at the corners of her mouth. It felt like the door to the cage she'd been living in her whole life had just been thrown open. When her friends told her that Greg was a fool for dumping her, she'd assumed they were just being kind. Her mother certainly hadn't bothered with that sentiment. She'd simply shaken her head and said that until Erin lowered her standards, she was bound to be disappointed by men.

But David made the comment with so much conviction, she believed every word of it. If a man like him found her attractive, what did the opinion of her two-timing ex-boyfriend matter anyway?

"Show me your scar," she said suddenly, then felt her eyes grow wide.

David looked as surprised at her request as she was at making it.

"I'm not sure that's such a grand plan, darlin'," he told her, his voice husky.

"Please," she whispered, hoping the magic word would have the same effect on him as it did on her. "I want to understand what happened to you."

"Isn't it enough to know I'm damaged goods?"

"You're not, and neither am I."

He lifted a brow. "Does that mean I get to see your breasts?"

Her mouth dropped open.

"I'm joking," he said, shrugging out of his jacket. "Although it's not such a bad idea now that I think about it. Best way to prove without a doubt that your ex-boyfriend was a total loser, don't you think?"

Erin swallowed. "I actually can't think right now."

David chuckled. "Then let's do this thing while your brain is jumbled." He grabbed the hem of his dark gray henley and pulled it over his head.

If Erin hadn't been able to think a moment ago, looking at David's gorgeous body made her feel like her mind had just been put in a blender. Every single one of her brain cells chose that moment to go on sabbatical, a fact that made the rest of her body sing with glee.

Because her body wanted things from this man that her brain couldn't handle. She knew David was big and broad, but she hadn't expected the golden skin or the darker hair that covered his chest. His body was all muscle, lean and toned and more delicious than anything she'd ever seen.

He moved, turning so she could see his beautiful back. The hard planes were just as pronounced, but at the top of his left shoulder was a pink scar about three inches long. It had clearly healed, but the color hadn't faded as much as she would have expected. The skin was raised where it had been sewn together.

"It's not pretty," he said over his shoulder. "They call it a keloid scar."

"That's why it's raised?"

"Yeah. They can do therapy to flatten it, but I never bothered. It's a reminder of how stupid and reckless I was."

Holding her breath, she reached out to run her fingertips along the ridge. His skin was warm, and she felt him stiffen under her touch.

"It's a good reminder that you're human," she told him. "Because otherwise you're a little too perfect."

"I'm far from perfect."

The feel of him mesmerized her. The fact that she was actually touching the man she'd had a crush on for months had sparks flying all through her body. "Hate to break it to you, but your body didn't get that message."

"You like my body?"

She snorted. "A ninety-year-old grandma would like your body."

"I've changed my mind." He moved so quickly all she had time to do was yelp, then she was in his arms with his heat enveloping her. "If I take off my clothes, you have to take off yours."

It was even more difficult to form a coherent thought with his chest hair tickling her cheek. She glanced to one side and—oh my—nipple at eye level.

She didn't even realize she'd licked her lips until David let out a soft groan. "Killing me here, darlin'. I can't even imagine what you're thinking, but I'm guessing it's dirty and I know I'd like it."

"Nothing I want to do to you is dirty," she said, trying to control her breathing. "People do it all the time. It's completely natural."

He lowered his head until his mouth skimmed hers. "What I want to do to you, Erin, is hot and dirty and no one can do it like me."

A volcano erupted inside her body. With just his words, David had her more aroused than she'd ever felt in her life. She brought a hand to her face and patted her cheek.

David smiled against her lips. "What are you doing?"

"Just making sure I didn't spontaneously combust."

He pulled back to gaze at her, his blue eyes warm and full of equal amounts of desire and amusement. "You're something special."

She opened her mouth to automatically correct him. No, she wasn't special. She was average. Ordinary. Boring.

But the way he looked at her made her *feel* special, so who was she to argue? "Fake it 'til you make it" had been her mantra during her first year of teaching, when she wasn't confident in her ability to handle a roomful of kindergartners.

The same principle applied now.

She reached up and fused her mouth to his, sliding her tongue along the seam of his lips. He rewarded her with a groan, and she felt it all the way to her toes. He lifted her until she was straddling him, her knees digging into the soft cushions of the couch.

She draped her arms around his neck and ran her fingers through his hair, every inch of her front plastered to the front of him. He deepened the kiss, making her senses reel. She wanted David with a thundering need that surpassed anything she'd felt before.

Her desire was so all-encompassing that she didn't even hesitate when he tugged at the hem of her cotton pajama top. She raised her arms and allowed him to pull it over her head, then gasped as his jaw grazed her breast.

"I'm not wearing a bra," she murmured, more to herself than him, suddenly remembering that she'd been tucked in bed reading when he'd knocked on her door.

"It's my lucky night," he said against her skin. His mouth closed around one nipple and Erin's body sang with joy. She gave herself over to the sensation of it, the gentle pressure and the sweet words he whispered as he held her.

He claimed her mouth again as his hand trailed under the waistband of her pants and into her panties. She whimpered when he dipped his fingers into her, the fire banking deep within her suddenly bursting into a million flames. He continued to kiss her, his tongue mimicking the motion of his fingers, and she exploded around him on a sharp cry.

It was like nothing she'd ever experienced and more than she would have guessed was possible, and she wanted the moment to last forever.

Chapter Nine

The sensation of Erin coming apart in his arms was pure bliss to David. From the tiny gasps of pleasure to her flushed skin to the way she cried out his name at the end, she was absolute perfection. It beat out the moment he was drafted by the Pirates, the first time he pitched a major-league game and so many wild nights with women he'd lost count. Which only made it that much more difficult to pull away.

Erin had gone pliant in his arms, soft and a little sleepy. He wanted nothing more than to finish what they'd started, to carry her to the bedroom and worship her body from head to toe. But she deserved better than an unplanned roll in the sheets.

She was worth more than she believed, and he was certain that taking her now was something they'd both come to regret.

He picked up her shirt and dropped it over her head.

She automatically pushed her arms through the sleeves, then frowned.

"What's going on?"

Her dark eyes were big and lovely and full of so much trust that he was sure to screw up in the end.

"I'm tucking you in," he said, grabbing his shirt from the floor, then moving one arm around her back and the other under her knees. He lifted her off the couch and started for the narrow hallway he assumed led to her bedroom.

She splayed her hand across his chest, her thumb just brushing one nipple, and he almost stumbled a step. "I'm not sleepy," she told him.

"It's late, Erin, and I didn't mean for things to go so far."

"So this was an accident?" Her eyes narrowed. "Or a mistake?"

He moved into the bedroom, where a lamp on the nightstand illuminated the space in a golden glow. She had a wrought iron bed frame with a patchwork quilt on top—both feminine and classic. Perfect for Erin.

As he lowered her onto the bed, which was unmade only on the side where she slept, he couldn't help but smile at the array of things spread across the quilt on the other side. There was an e-reader with a polka-dot cover, several paperback books, a box of tissues and…

"You have a cat?"

She darted a glance to the ball of fur that didn't so much as offer a tail flick to acknowledge that people had entered its space. "That's Sugar. She's kind of standoffish until she gets to know you."

"See," he said, dropping a kiss on the top of her head, "there's no room for me in the bed anyway." He gestured to the stack of books as he pulled on his henley. "You have too many heroes already."

"You're placating me," she told him, "and I don't like it. That was—" she pointed toward the family room "—pretty darn awesome for me. Beyond awesome. I'm grateful, but I also understand if I don't do it for you. Just man up and tell me."

He grabbed her wrists, pinned them above her head and leaned in to take her mouth, allowing all the frustration and need pounding through his body to transfer to the kiss.

Maybe he was trying to freak her out, to prove that what he wanted was surely more than she was willing to give. Instead, she met his desire with her own, and it tore through him like a brush fire, igniting every part of him until he had to force himself to release her again.

"I want you, Erin. I want us. I want to start with all night, and keep going for as long as you'll let me."

She drew in a breath, pressed her fingertips to lips swollen from his kiss. "Then why..."

"I'm not exactly a stand-up guy, but I know when a woman deserves more than I can give. When I told you I wanted to court you, it wasn't a joke. I want you to feel special—"

"Mission accomplished on the couch."

"I want you to understand how special you are. I wish you saw yourself the way I see you." He straightened, shook his head. "I have to admit I didn't think you'd accept my apology tonight, and I wouldn't have blamed you in the least."

"I'll find another way to get funding," she said, but he could hear the hesitation in her voice. He wanted to kick himself for how he'd acted earlier. He'd spent his whole life dealing with losers like Joel Martin, and had been in more than his share of fights to defend his sister. But he was older now, and he should be smarter. He had Rhett to think about.

And now Erin.

More than anything, David wanted to be the type of man who would deserve her.

"I'll help you," he told her.

"You don't have to—"

"Let me help you."

She gave him a shy smile. "Okay."

"And let me take you out on a real date." When she didn't respond immediately, he added a soft, "Please."

"You're pretty good with manners," she told him, rolling her eyes.

"I'm good with a lot of things." He leaned in and gave her one last lingering kiss. "I plan to demonstrate every one of my skills for you."

To his surprise, she laughed. The sound loosened the invisible band that stretched tight around his heart. "Are you sure you don't read romance novels? Because that sounds like the perfect hero line to me."

"No hero here," he told her. "But I hope you have some sweet dreams tonight."

"Good night, David," she whispered.

"Good night, Erin."

By the beginning of the following week, Erin wondered if she'd dreamed her whole encounter with David.

A sweet dream, indeed, but disappointing to think she'd made the whole thing up in her head.

What other explanation could there be for the fact that she hadn't seen or heard from him in five days? She might not be an expert on courting, but there was no doubt that's not how it typically went.

Each day, regret plagued her. The more plausible explanations for David's silence were a lot harder to take. Maybe she shouldn't have let things go so far on her couch. It felt like he put her up on some pedestal she wasn't interested in standing on, so could it be possible that he'd lost respect for her? The more logical reason was simply that he wasn't interested yet didn't want to hurt her feelings.

Which hurt her more than if he'd been honest in the first place.

She'd thought he might ask her out for the previous weekend, and she'd been fool enough to check her cell phone compulsively most of Saturday, waiting for a call that never came. In the end, she'd ordered pizza and binge-watched *Pride and Prejudice*—both the BBC and Hollywood versions. Then she'd thrown in *Bridget Jones's Diary* for an extra Colin Firth fix.

She told herself she should get in the habit of keeping her books on her nightstand instead of the other side of the bed. But really, why bother when Sugar was the one sharing it?

Rhett had been making progress with his social skills, playing with Elaina during recess and interacting with the other kids in the after-school program.

Joel Martin hadn't been back to see her, but Isaac's mother, Danielle, had signed him up for the program on the two days when she worked until five at the Hair Nation salon outside of town. Other than a subtle side-eye toward Rhett, the woman had been polite and grateful to have a place for her son to go after school.

Isaac and Rhett had seemed to silently agree to a truce. The funny thing was the boys had a lot in common. Both were slow to make friends but craved social interactions. They liked building things and games of any sort. She'd managed to engage them both in a puzzle Monday afternoon and wished their parents could handle things so maturely.

It was nearly five on Tuesday when an older woman with thick blond hair piled high on her head and makeup applied to make her look ten years younger sauntered into the room.

"Rhett, baby," she called, "get your things. Nana's taking you out for a special treat."

Rhett looked up from where he was making a race car out of modeling clay. "I'm 'posed to stay here until Uncle David comes to get me. He's picking me up."

"Change of plans," the woman said. She moved forward and adjusted her oversize purse on her shoulder. "I'm Angela McCay, Rhett's grandma."

Erin felt color rush to her face at the way Angela's gaze seemed to take her in and automatically dismiss her. "David mentioned you arrived in town."

Angela's blue eyes turned assessing. "Oh, did he now?" She shrugged. "I don't think he talked about you. Are you and my son close?"

"Um…we know each other because of Rhett." If David hadn't mentioned her, she wasn't going to give this woman any details of her relationship—if she could even call it that.

Rhett came to stand next to Erin. "I told you Ms. MacDonald is my favorite teacher."

"You're in kindergarten," Angela said, reaching out a hand to tousle Rhett's blond hair. "There isn't a lot to compare her to."

"She's still my favorite," Rhett said, his small chin jutting out.

Erin felt a flood of gratitude for the boy and his innocent loyalty.

"Do I need to sign something to check him out?" Angela asked, ignoring Rhett's comment.

"Each parent or guardian submits a form naming the people approved to pick up their child from the program." Erin tried not to fidget under Angela's stare. She could see where David and his sister got their looks.

Angela might be a little rough around the edges, but it was clear she must have been a traffic-stopping beauty in her day. Lines snaked out from the edges of her eyes and around her mouth, but she still had high cheekbones, bee-stung lips and the kind of figure that seemed out of place on a woman with a five-year-old grandson.

She wore a long-sleeved white T-shirt, low-slung jeans and boots. Around her neck were several strands of turquoise layered on top of a couple of heavy silver chains.

"I'm his nana," the woman said, her tone icy. "Of course I have permission to pick him up."

Erin pressed her fingers to the place on her chest where a knot of nerves was forming. "If you'd wait a minute, I'll call David to confirm."

Just then one of the third-grade boys lobbed a purple crayon across the table at one of his friends. Instead of its intended target, the crayon hit the water cup a threesome of girls was sharing as they painted. The dirty water spilled across the table, sending the girls into a screaming panic.

"It's okay, girls," Erin said, holding up a finger to ask Rhett's grandmother to wait a moment. "We can clean things up."

"Are you in charge of all these kids?" Angela asked over the din.

"I have help," Erin answered, trying not to sound defensive, "but she went down to the office to make copies."

"Looks like you've bitten off a little more than you can chew."

Embarrassment rushed through Erin. The old adage was one of her mother's favorite reminders from when Erin was a girl. Every time Erin wanted to sign up for a new activity or try out for a team, her mother had said, "Don't bite off more than you can chew."

She hurried over to the side table and grabbed a roll of paper towels. "I've got it under control."

"While you deal with—" Angela waved her hands at the mess "—I'm going to take Rhett."

"I really need to talk to—"

"My new shirt," one of the girls screeched. "Paint water's ruining my new shirt."

"Honey, let me make this easy on you." Angela reached out and took Rhett's hand. "I'll text my son and let him know the boy's with me. You take care of your mess."

"It's not a mess," Erin muttered at the same moment one of the girls, Ava Elliott, punched the boy who'd thrown the crayon in the stomach.

Erin hurried to them as the boy doubled over in pain.

By the time she looked up again, Angela and Rhett were gone.

Claire Travers, the teenager who was assisting her with the program, came back in the room, her eyes growing wide at the chaos and commotion. "I was gone for like five minutes," she said.

"It's fine," Erin called. "Get Ava and Paige cleaned up, okay?"

She helped the boy who'd been punched, Fletcher, to a seat on the beanbag.

"Can't breathe," he whispered on a gasp.

"She knocked the wind out of you." Erin smoothed his hair away from his face. "Look at me and concentrate on moving air in—" she took a breath "—and out," she said on an exhale.

Fletcher swiped a hand over his eyes and did what she said. After a few minutes he was breathing normally.

Claire managed to calm the girls and soon everything was back under control. Erin grabbed her phone to text David about his mother just at the same time parents started arriving to pick up kids. She meant to get back to the text, but as the last child walked out with her mother, Sara Travers poked her head into the room.

"So this is where the child-wrangling magic happens?" she asked.

"I helped manage a full-blown meltdown today with a couple of the girls," Claire proudly told her stepmother.

"She was brilliant," Erin confirmed, feeling slightly awkward under Sara's gorgeous blue gaze. Sara had been a famous child actor before her career got derailed in her teens. She'd come to Crimson a few years ago, fallen in love with Josh Travers and helped him open the Crimson Ranch guest ranch. Since then, her career had made a resurgence and now she balanced her Hollywood life with her life in the mountains.

Although Erin didn't know her personally, she'd seen Sara around town quite a bit. With Crimson's proximity to Aspen, she should be used to movie star sightings, but it felt different with Sara. She was an integral part of the community after having lived in Crimson only a few years. Erin was still skirting the sidelines even though she'd spent most of her life in town.

Olivia, who was Claire's aunt by marriage, had arranged for the girl to assist Erin in the afternoons. Erin still hoped to receive funding to expand the program and her staff. Until then, Claire was a huge help. The girl was only fifteen but already had an instinctive talent for connecting with young kids.

"Way to go, Claire-bear," Sara said, giving the girl a quick hug. Although she wore a casual pair of distressed jeans with an oversize sweater, she still managed to project a look of subtle glamour. "You're amazing."

The girl rolled her eyes like a typical teenager, but Erin could tell the simple praise meant a lot to her. It seemed to come so easily, and not for the first time Erin wondered what it would have been like to grow up in a household where she'd been valued instead of constantly found lacking.

"Your dad is waiting downstairs," Sara told Claire. "The truck is parked at the curb. We thought we'd grab dinner in town. Why don't you head on down?"

Claire smiled at Erin. "I'll see you tomorrow?"

"I count on it," Erin answered. "I really appreciate your help, Claire."

The girl disappeared through the open doorway.

"She's special," Erin said to Sara.

"I wanted to tell you how much Josh and I appreciate you giving her this opportunity. She loves kids, and has plenty of experience babysitting, but this is different."

Erin gave a small laugh. "Not too different some days."

Sara inclined her head. "When did you know you wanted to be a teacher?"

Erin thought about how to answer the question. She'd played school with her stuffed animals as a young girl, then been the one to ask teachers if she could help with the younger kids at recess as she'd gotten older. But she'd also known being a teacher wouldn't be enough to satisfy her mom, so she'd feigned interest in a variety of more high-profile careers until she'd gone to college and immediately switched her major from premed to elementary education.

"My mother," she said, keeping her tone neutral, "was very much of the belief that 'those who can, do, and those who can't, teach.'"

Sara groaned softly.

"I think I knew—or at least recognized that I liked working with kids—for most of my life. All of my pretend play centered around setting up classrooms for my dolls and stuffed animals."

"I didn't have much of a childhood," Sara said, surprising Erin with her candor. "I was the breadwinner in the family, and whether or not I wanted to act, that was what I had to do."

"Would you have chosen something else if you'd had the chance?" Erin couldn't help but ask.

"Maybe," Sara said with a shrug. "Something normal where I could just be a regular person."

Erin blinked. She'd spent her whole life wanting to be something other than regular. Now a famous actress stood in front of her wishing for normal.

"I've got the best of both worlds now. But I don't want Claire to go through what I did..." Sara paused, then added, "Or what you did as she tries to figure out her path in life."

"She's young and obviously quite intelligent." Erin straightened a stack of papers on the desk, then pulled her purse out of a drawer. "She's lucky to have people in her life who want to support her. She'd be an excellent teacher, and I'm sure she'll succeed in whatever she chooses to do with her life."

Sara drew in an audible breath. "Will you record that so I can play it back to her when the teenage drama and doubts get to be too much?"

"Keep her engaged and stay involved in her life. I know you're busy and have plenty of important things to take care of, but if you ever want to come with Claire, I can always use more hands on deck."

Sara's already huge eyes widened further. She looked around the room, then back to Erin. "Would that be weird? I'm not great with kids. I mean, I was one and I have Claire and Emery, but she's a baby. She can't talk."

"My kids like to talk," Erin said with a smile. "Especially when they have people to listen to them. You're an actress. I'm sure you can fake it."

"I faked it for a lot of years," Sara said, then laughed. "I'm an expert."

"Tell me about it," Erin muttered. It was strange to feel this camaraderie with a woman whose life was so different, but comforting at the same time.

"I'll let you get on with your evening," Sara said, stepping forward to envelop Erin in a quick hug. Sara's fragrance was subtle and earthy but clearly expensive, and Erin couldn't wait to tell her friends she'd been hugged by the A-list actress. "We should get together some time. A bunch of us have regular get-togethers—mostly for Mexican and margaritas but sometimes coffee or yoga. I'll call you before the next one and you can join us."

"Thank you," Erin whispered, feeling better than she had in a long time.

As Sara turned to leave, David rushed into the room. "Sorry I'm late. We were having trouble with fermenting the most recent batch of the wheat beer."

"Hey, David." Sara smiled. "I'm looking forward to watching you win the big prize in a couple of weeks."

"If we sort through the problems with this latest batch, maybe I'll actually have a beer to enter."

"Good luck," Sara said with a grin, and walked out of the room.

"Thanks." He ran a hand through his hair, then turned to Erin. "Where's Rhett?"

"With your mother," she said, her stomach dropping at the way his brows drew down. "She was supposed to call you."

Pulling his phone out of his pocket, he shook his head. "No texts or calls."

"She told me—"

"I thought you weren't supposed to send him home with random people. Isn't that why I filled out the paperwork?"

"His grandmother isn't random," Erin insisted, even though she'd given the same argument to Angela. "She wanted to take him out for a fun afternoon."

David muttered a curse under his breath then said, "You don't want to know my mother's definition of fun."

"I thought she was here helping," Erin said, throwing up her hands. "She's staying with you. You don't trust her with Rhett?"

"I trust her." David paced to the edge of the room. "Sort of. But she's been talking about taking him up the mountain to see the leaves changing. I told her she had to stay in town with him, and we got in an argument about it. My mom is flighty and reckless. For all I know, she'll start a hike with him and lose him in the woods."

"No," Erin whispered. "That's not possible."

"She took Jenna and me to downtown Pittsburgh one year for a Christmas parade. She got sidetracked by some sale at a department store and left us on the street with instructions not to move. Apparently, she forgot that she was doing more than a shopping trip and went home. The police finally picked us up after a street sweeper called them. According to my mom, she thought we were playing in the backyard."

"David."

"It was below freezing," he said, almost as an afterthought. "Just like it gets cold up on the mountain at night this time of year."

Erin shook her head. "That can't be what's happened. I bet she went for an ice cream. If you said not to leave—"

"My mom doesn't give a—" He clamped his mouth shut. "She means well and she's been fine this time around, but she's not always reliable. Not when it counts."

"David, I'm—"

He held up a hand. "It's not your fault. I believed she'd changed. I needed to believe because it's what Jenna wanted and I have no clue what I'm doing with a five-year-old boy."

"You're handling things like a pro," she said, reaching out a hand to squeeze his arm and trying not to take it personally when he shrugged off her touch.

"Clearly, this night is a great example of that." He hit a button on his phone. "Maybe I'll get lucky and she'll pick up."

Erin waited, hoping with every fiber of her being Angela answered. A moment later, David took the phone away from his ear and shook his head. "Straight to voice mail. She's either ignoring me or out of cell range."

"A text might go through," Erin suggested quietly.

He punched in a message, hit Send, and they waited again. David's full mouth pressed into a thin line. "I've got to call Cole and see if he has any deputies up on the mountain. It's going to get dark soon, and I need to know Rhett is okay."

"I'm sorry," she whispered, feeling miserable.

"It's not your problem," he answered even as he continued to stare at the phone. "You're just the teacher."

Erin swallowed. She knew he hadn't meant the words as an insult. He was stressed and worried. But just as he'd wanted to believe in his mother, Erin had wanted to believe in him. In the two of them. He'd said he'd wanted her. Wanted "us."

But once again, she wasn't enough.

He turned away when Cole picked up, and she could hear him explaining the situation to the sheriff. After a minute, he faced her again. "He's going to check out some of the more popular driving routes for viewing the changing leaves. I'm going to look around town to see if they're down here, then head up myself."

"Will you text me when you find them?"

He studied her as if weighing his answer, then finally nodded.

"How can I help?"

"You can't," he whispered, then walked away.

Chapter Ten

The sun had set over the craggy peak of Crimson Mountain, and the sky was aflame in shades of pink and orange as Erin took a curve on the two-lane highway that led up the mountain. Within a half hour, the whole mountainside would be cast in shadow, so there wasn't much time for an effective search.

Her heart felt like it was breaking when David said he didn't need her, but she refused to let that stop her from trying to find Rhett and Angela.

It had been almost an hour since he'd walked away from her, so maybe David had tracked them down by now and hadn't bothered to text her. Erin couldn't take the chance. She was done sitting on the sidelines letting life pass her by, especially when she'd been the cause of the mess they were in.

There were so many service roads and gravel offshoots of the main highway it was difficult to know where to start. Obviously, Cole Bennett and his team of deputies were experts, and she hadn't even thought to ask David what kind of car his mother drove. But Erin had some experience on these roads. She'd always loved the changing colors that swathed the mountains. For a few weeks, the brilliant patches of bright yellow aspens and a few orange and red clumps of scrub oak made the whole valley look like it was on fire.

She turned her car onto a dirt road that led to one of the most picturesque vistas overlooking the valley. It wasn't quite as popular as some of the well-known leaf-viewing drives in the area but remained a favorite with locals.

Angela wasn't a local, but if she'd stopped at the hardware store or the gas station on the west side of town, this was where they would have sent her.

Erin ignored the gorgeous scenery surrounding her and concentrated on scanning the edges of the road and the myriad pull-offs that led to private cabins or trailhead access for hiking.

It was a little bit like searching for a needle in a haystack. When she darted a quick glance at her phone she realized she was out of service range. So even if David had tracked down Rhett and texted her, she wouldn't get the message.

The car climbed almost to tree-line level, Erin growing more frustrated by the second. Why had she allowed Angela to take Rhett? The answer was clear—Erin didn't have enough faith in herself or her authority to stop the other woman. Which was stupid, because of all the things Erin had been too scared of failing at to try, working with kids had never been one of them.

She was a great teacher, and her after-school program was already making a difference. Two of the teachers at school had reported that their students—the ones who'd been identified as troublemakers—were less disruptive and more responsible in class. The kids had cited some of the self-directed exercises for regulating behavior Erin had taught them for the changes.

No matter what her mother thought…or Angela…or David…or her ex…she had value. Maybe if she started believing that about herself, other people would, too.

She was about to turn the car around and head down the hillside when she caught sight of an older-model sedan parked on the side of the road about two hundred yards in front of her.

Adrenaline spiked through her when she noticed the Pennsylvania license plate. As she approached, the driver's-side door opened and Angela stepped out, her pale blond hair shining in the waning light.

Erin breathed a huge sigh of relief as she pulled her Subaru to a stop behind Angela's car. She checked her phone—still no service, but as soon as they got back into cell range she could let David know Rhett was safe.

"Stupid car battery gave out," Angela said sullenly. "And I've got no service up here. We've got satellite radio that can play music anywhere in the dang world. Don't you think they could get some decent coverage for phones?"

Rhett jumped out of the car through the open door. "Ms. MacDonald, you found us."

"Your uncle is worried," Erin said, crouching down to wrap her arms around the boy's shoulders as he ran to her.

"Since when did my son become a worrywart?" Angela retrieved her purse from the front seat of the car and slammed the door shut. "I texted him a message that Rhett and I were getting ice cream and going to look at leaves."

"He never got a message from you," Erin said, feeling defensive on David's behalf. "You promised you'd get in touch with him if I let you take Rhett today."

"Let me?" Angela scoffed. "I'm his grandma and I'll take him—"

"No." Holding tight to Rhett's hand, Erin stepped forward. "When Rhett is at school or with me in the afternoon, he's my responsibility. Unless you have permission from David, I won't allow you to pick him up again."

Angela studied her through narrowed eyes. "Is that so? You do realize my daughter is the one who called and asked me to drive halfway across the country to look out for her boy?"

Erin felt Rhett stiffen beside her. "Rhett," she said, gently taking him by the shoulders, "you should get in my car. It's cold out here. We'll take the booster seat from your grandma's—"

"Nana doesn't have a booster," he interrupted quietly.

"We'll make sure she gets one," she told him. "Your nana and I have a few things to work out and then we'll go find Uncle David."

Biting his lip, the boy looked between Angela and Erin, then headed for the car.

"I'm his grandmother," the older woman repeated as Rhett shut the door.

"I appreciate that." Erin forced her shoulders back and her hands at her side. "I know Jenna is working through her issues, and I understand you're here to help. David does, as well. But he's in charge, Angela. He's balancing so much and trying to do his best by Rhett."

"Sounds like you know my son pretty well." Angela gave her another once-over but before she could continue, Erin held up a hand.

"I hope David and I are friends, but even if we're not, I care about Rhett. He's a great kid and I want to see him through this. We all do." She stepped forward. "I'm not the enemy, Angela. Neither is David."

She saw the woman's shoulders deflate slightly. "Do you know what happened to Jenna when they were in high school?"

Erin shook her head. "I don't, and it's none of my business if David doesn't want to tell me." As much as she wanted to know.

"You should ask him before you get too close."

At Angela's words, a sinking feeling rippled through Erin. Whatever had happened to his sister in high school clearly formed the man David was today. Erin might not know any details, but she understood it must have been traumatic.

"My son is not the type of man who's good for a woman like you." Angela reached out and, to Erin's surprise, patted her softly on the arm. "Rhett is lucky to have you in his life." She took a deep breath, then added, "He's lucky to have David, too. I'm freezing my fanny off up here now that the sun is gone. Let's get back to town so I can make this right with my son."

Erin nodded and they headed to the car. The drive was quiet until they got into cell phone range. Angela's phone was still dead, but Erin's gave several insistent chirps. She took the phone from the console and handed it to David's mother. "You call since I'm driving."

Out of the corner of her eye, Erin saw Angela smile as she looked at the phone.

"What's so funny?"

"You have my son in your contacts."

"Yes."

"His occupation is listed as 'hottie brewmaster.' Is that an official title?"

Erin suppressed a groan. Melody had entered that into her phone, and Erin had forgotten to change it.

"You're stalling," she said as an answer. "Call him."

With a small laugh, Angela hit the button to dial David. After a minute she said, "This is your mother. We're on our way back to town. I left you…" She was quiet for a moment. Erin could hear the muffled rumble of David's voice through the phone but couldn't make out what he was saying. Based on the furrow between Angela's brows, it wasn't good.

"She drove up the mountain and found us," Angela said. Another pause. "It's not my fault the wreck of a car I drive died. Rhett is fine."

"I'm hungry," Rhett called from the back seat.

"He's hungry," Angela repeated, then went silent again as David said something else. "What's that?" She made the sound of static. "Sorry, you're breaking up. We'll see you at home in a bit."

Erin arched a brow as Angela disconnected the call. "Faking a bad connection?"

The older woman shrugged. "He has all night to rip me a new one. I'd like a few minutes of quiet to gather my wits." She pressed her hands to her cheeks. "For the record, my plan was to get a treat and see the leaves, not to get stuck up on the mountain in the cold at dusk."

A rush of emotion flooded Erin when Angela's voice cracked. Despite the attitude, Erin realized David's mother had been more scared than she'd let on to be stranded with Rhett. Erin reached across the console and patted the woman's leg. "It all turned out okay in the end."

"Thank you," Angela whispered and squeezed Erin's fingers.

"Wonder what Uncle David will make for dinner," Rhett said from the back seat. "I'm so hungry even his cooking will taste good tonight."

Erin laughed and was once again reminded how resilient kids could be. "We'll soon find out," she told Rhett, and concentrated on getting them home safely.

David's heart clamored in his chest as he waited on the sidewalk in front of Elevation, and the unfamiliar feeling sent shock waves through him. When was the last time he'd been so worried? The past hour had been the longest of his life. After talking to his mother, he'd gotten in touch with Cole, who had been on the mountain searching for Rhett.

As much as it killed him, David had kept close to town, wanting to remain reachable by his mother if she called. He'd never expected Erin to be conducting her own search, let alone to find his mother and Rhett—especially not after how he'd treated her.

He massaged the back of his neck with one hand. He had the uncanny ability to continuously push away the one person who was quickly coming to mean the most to him.

A small Subaru hatchback pulled to the curb in front of the bar. His mother opened the passenger door at the same time Rhett bounded out from the back seat. David opened his arms, catching the boy and spinning him around.

"Nana's car broke," Rhett said into his neck. "And I'm hungry. Did you make dinner?"

"Even better." David kissed the top of the boy's head and dropped him back down to the ground. "The cook at Elevation made you mac and cheese."

"Mac and cheese," Rhett shouted happily. "Nana, did you hear? Uncle David didn't cook!"

His mother smiled at Rhett. "It's your lucky night." She held out her hand. "Come on. Let's go upstairs."

"I got to get my backpack," Rhett said and turned for the car again.

It was then David realized Erin had also gotten out of

the car and now stood at the edge of the sidewalk. His knees almost gave way from the feeling of longing that charged through him. He wanted to rush forward and enfold her in his arms, somehow knowing that if he held her, his world would fall into place.

Her dark hair was uncharacteristically down, curling over her shoulders and the light jacket she wore. The coat wasn't enough to stave off the cold, and he saw her shiver as a gust of wind whipped down the street. She held out the small Ninja Turtles backpack to Rhett. "Here you go, sweetie."

"Thanks for rescuing us, Ms. MacDonald," Rhett said as he grabbed the pack.

"I'm glad you're safe. See you tomorrow at school."

"Thank you," his mother added, and Erin gave her a little wave. Then Angela and Rhett disappeared through the door that led up to the apartment.

"Erin." David stepped forward, but she held up a hand. "Go take care of Rhett."

"You found them."

"I know you didn't want me involved, but I couldn't just walk away. Don't be too hard on your mother. She's more shaken up by this than she lets on."

He blinked. "Are you defending my mother?"

"I guess I am. She's trying, David. We're all trying. Tonight was my fault for letting her take him without your permission." She laughed softly, then added, "But you know that already."

"No." He reached for her wrist and spun her to him when she turned away. "I'm sorry about the things I said." He brushed his fingers across her cheek. Darkness had officially fallen and her skin glowed under the light of the streetlamps. "I'm sorry my go-to emotion is anger.

It's been that way for a long time, Erin. I don't know how to change it."

She looked up at him through her lashes. "Do you want it to change?"

"For Rhett, yes." He pressed his forehead to hers and whispered. "For you, yes." There was no way to put into words all the things he'd change for this woman if he could. "Why couldn't we have met when my life was simple?"

He felt rather than saw her smile. "Exactly when was your life simple?"

"Third grade," he answered without hesitation. "I had a crush on Brandi Doerger. I chased her around the playground until she agreed to be my girlfriend. Then I kissed her under the flagpole."

She pulled back enough to look at him. "Where is Brandi now?"

"Ours was a short-lived romance."

"And why is that?"

He shrugged. "She wanted me to meet at the candy store across from school and buy her favorite candy bar to prove I was her boyfriend."

"You didn't have the money for a gift?"

"I had a baseball game to get to with my friends."

"So you stood the poor girl up?"

"I was the pitcher," he said, hoping that explained everything. When he was nine, it seemed like a good enough excuse, but as something like disappointment flashed in Erin's gaze, he realized that nothing in his life had ever been simple.

"You don't have anything to prove to me." She untangled herself from his embrace and walked to her car.

He glanced up to his apartment windows and knew he

had to see to Rhett and talk to his mother. But he couldn't let Erin leave like this. Not again.

"Give me another chance," he called.

She stilled in the midst of opening her door and turned to face him. "Why do you even want one?"

A group of twentysomethings was walking toward Elevation and a couple of them hooted with laughter at her question. "She's gonna roast you, dude," one of the taller guys said, slapping David on the arm as he walked by and into the restaurant.

Had he ever been that young and carefree? No, he'd been young and disastrously stupid.

"Because," he said, ignoring everything except Erin's brown eyes, "nothing in my life makes sense right now except you."

He stepped closer but still respected the space she'd put between them. As much as he wanted to push her to let him in despite what a jerk he'd been. It had to be her choice. Never in his life had he wanted a woman to choose him as much as he did now. "Even though I keep finding ways to screw it up, I want you."

Her fingers tightened on her purse strap, as if there was a debate raging inside her brain. It would be the smart thing to walk away from him right now. He sure as hell hoped she wasn't going to do the smart thing.

"Can you define another chance?"

He wanted to pump his fist in the air. She was watching out for herself, but she hadn't said a straight-up *no.* He had a chance, but he had to work for it. David might have made a lot of mistakes in his life, but he could work for something he wanted.

"A real date."

"I've heard that offer before," she countered. "Yet here we are."

Right.

Although he knew how to work, he'd never needed to try to get a woman. "Saturday," he continued. "All day. I'll pick you up at noon."

"What about Rhett?"

David must be more out of practice with women than he even realized. The fact that her first question was about his nephew made his heart clench in ways he didn't want to examine.

"I'll work it out."

She bit down on her lip as her gaze skittered away. "I don't want to force you to take me out. I wasn't lying when I said you have nothing to prove to me. You don't owe me a—"

"I do have something to prove. I need to prove that I'm not the guy I keep showing myself to be. Go out with me, Erin. Please."

She took a deep breath, then met his gaze again. "Do you know I'm a sucker for the word *please*?" she asked, her tone almost annoyed.

He laughed softly. "I didn't before now, but you can bet I'm going to use it to my advantage."

"I'll see you at noon on Saturday," she whispered.

"You'll see me this week," he corrected, "with Rhett. But Saturday is going to be special."

"Can I ask what we're doing?"

"You can ask, but I won't tell. I'm going to wow you. Just wait."

She rolled her eyes and muttered something that sounded like, "If you only knew."

With a small wave, she got in her car and pulled out of her parking spot and down the street.

David glanced up at the apartment windows again but before he went upstairs, took a quick detour into Elevation.

Tracie was tending bar, and he grabbed her shoulders and spun her to face him. "I need to impress a woman," he said. "With a date."

"Take off your shirt," one of the women sitting at the bar told him. He turned to see three women who looked vaguely familiar staring at him. He thought he recognized them from dropping off Rhett at school. Great. Now he was going to be known as the incompetent guardian who couldn't handle women.

Had he really just asked Tracie for dating advice in the middle of his bar?

Two of the women giggled, then the blonde with a short bob leaned forward. "My divorce was final last week." She winked. "I think you're damn impressive just standing there so—"

"Enough," Tracie interrupted the woman, and waved over the new bartender she'd hired to work evenings while David was with Rhett. "Hey, Mark, will you pour these three lovelies a round on the house? No need for the ego-stroking, ladies. I'll take it from here."

She pushed David toward the end of the bar. "What in the hell are you talking about? From the stories I've heard, you went out with half the single women in Pennsylvania in your day. Why do you suddenly need dating advice?"

David gripped the edge of the bar, almost wishing he was still the hot-tempered young baseball phenom who could get away with throwing a fist through the wall. "I asked Erin out."

Tracie stared at him for several moments, then prompted, "And..."

"I told her it was going to be special."

"So make reservations at some swanky place in Aspen," Tracie told him. "I know beer is your thing, but you do remember how to pay for expensive food and wine, right?"

"I need to wow her."

She held up her hands. "Dude, if you're looking for bedroom advice—"

"No," he said quickly. "But Erin is a…a…"

"A woman?"

He blew out a breath. "A lady. I'm not trying to wine and dine her to get into her pants."

One side of Tracie's mouth curved. "You don't want in her pants?"

"Of course I want—" He stopped, growled under his breath. "She's special. I don't want to screw it up. Any guy with a phone and credit card can make a reservation. I need it to be something more."

"I've never seen you like this, boss." She shook her head. "Thank God."

"Forget it."

She laughed, then chucked him on the arm. "I've got an idea. But your prim and proper teacher lady is into you. You know that. I know that. It's a small town, and the school district set likes Elevation. I've seen the way she looks at you when she's here with her friends, and that was before Rhett."

"I never noticed her."

"Because men are idiots." Tracie tsked. "My point is that she's kind of…a sure thing. She crushed on you hard."

"I still need to earn it." He leaned in closer. "Help me. Please."

Tracie rolled her blue eyes to the ceiling. "I bet that sad puppy-dog face and the *please* work on her every time."

"Kind of," he admitted.

"That girl and I need to spend some time together." The new bartender called to Tracie as a line formed in front of the bar. "I've got to get back to work," Tracie said, giving him one of her patented smirks. "Don't want the boss to catch me slacking. I'll come in tomorrow after my run and we can plan world domination—or at least kindergarten teacher domination."

"That sounds kinky."

"You never know," she called over her shoulder as she headed back to the bar. "That might be how she likes it."

David's mind started to wander to an image of Erin dressed in nothing but—

He slapped his palm against his forehead several times. That kind of daydreaming wasn't going to get the five-year-old boy waiting upstairs bathed and ready for bed or his mother dealt with in any sort of productive way.

After scanning the interior of the bar one more time to make sure things were under control, he headed for his apartment. He had to keep things on track this week. He had one more chance with Erin, and he wasn't going to blow it.

Chapter Eleven

"I've never heard of a therapy rabbit." Erin watched in wonder as her Kidzone students took turns petting the bunny that happily hopped up to each of them on the activity rug.

"Fritzi is special." She glanced at Caden Sharpe, the local rancher who also ran an animal rescue center out of his property, his hard features suddenly surprisingly gentle.

Emily Whitaker Crenshaw, the mom of one of Erin's former students, had suggested she call Caden. His manner was gruff, and Erin had been certain he'd refuse her request to bring the kids to his ranch. Instead, he not only set up a time for them to visit but also offered to stop by the community center with a couple of the animals he'd trained as therapy pets.

Caden had been a few years ahead of her in school and had been so surly and mean as a boy she'd barely had the nerve to make eye contact with him. She'd heard rumors that his early life had been tough and wealthy rancher Garrett Sharpe had adopted him when he was ten years old. But even the stable home and the brothers he'd gained in his new family hadn't seemed to settle his restless spirit.

He reminded her of some of the kids she worked with and hoped that meeting Caden, who was also an army vet, would help them realize they had other paths available to them.

Although right now Fritzi the bunny and Otis, the yellow Lab enjoying belly rubs from a group of girls, were the real stars of the show.

"You're doing good work here," Caden told her. Erin realized those were the most words she'd heard the man string together in a sentence.

"I sometimes think I'm in over my head," she admitted. "But as amazing as this community is, there was a need for these kids that wasn't being filled. There are too many who have the potential to get into trouble if no one is watching out for them."

He shifted slightly and she colored under his intense gaze. "I wasn't talking about you."

A noise came from him that might have been a laugh, but it was rough like it had been closed in a drawer and forgotten for too long. "I remember you now," he said. "You were always smiling."

Erin felt her blush deepen. "Did you know that smiling can reduce your blood pressure? Plus it's an easy gift to offer another person."

"People used to be afraid to smile at me."

She raised a brow. "I think that's how you liked it."

He laughed again. "Maybe. The animals help with that."

She gave him her brightest smile. "Thank you for

bringing them here and the invitation to visit the ranch. It will mean a lot to the kids."

He studied her for another long moment. "Would you want—"

A flash of movement over his shoulder caught her eye and she realized David was standing in the door watching the exchange.

"Come on in," she called, glancing at her watch. "I didn't realize it had gotten so late."

"I'm a few minutes early," David said. As he walked toward her, his hand came around from behind his back and she realized he held a bouquet of roses. "These are for you."

"Oh." She pressed a hand to her chest. "No one has ever brought me flowers who wasn't one of my students." She wrapped her hand around the stems, her fingers brushing his. The current of awareness between them zinged to life and she had to fight to remember they were standing in front of ten kids, as well as Caden Sharpe.

"You should have them all the time," David told her.

She heard a sound that might have been a growl come from Caden, but when she turned he was simply watching the kids and the animals.

"Do you two know each other?" she asked, lowering her nose close to the flower petals and inhaling the fresh scent.

"We've met," David answered. "I get all my beef from Sharpe Pointe Ranch."

"Yep," was Caden's only response.

"Great." She glanced between the two men and wondered why it felt like there was some invisible swordplay going on. "Caden brought his animals to visit with the kids."

"I brought flowers," David said immediately.

She nodded slowly. "Um, yes, you did. And I love them."

David leaned a little closer to Caden. "She loves them."

A muscle ticked in Caden's jaw. "I'm going to round up Fritzi and Otis," he told her. "I'll see you when you bring the kids to the ranch. You're welcome any time."

"I definitely will. Thank you."

She watched him turn to David. "She's going to call me," he said under his breath.

David's shoulders stiffened but before he could respond, Erin placed the flowers on her desk and clapped her hands to get the kids' attention. The noise level was surprisingly low given how excited the kids had been to see the bunny and dog. But she had to admit there was something inherently relaxing about the energy of the two animals. She sensed that with Caden as well, despite his gruff demeanor, and was happy he'd found a purpose in life.

"It's time for the animals to go," she announced to a round of groans. "But Mr. Sharpe has invited us out to his ranch for a longer visit." That got some cheers from the kids. "Can you give him a big thank-you for coming to see us today?"

Caden seemed embarrassed by the attention, and left quickly after packing up the bunny and putting Otis on a leash. Parents started to arrive soon after for pickup, and she waved as David led Rhett from the room.

Soon only Isaac remained, and he sat at one of the small craft tables, his head bent forward.

"Your mom will be here soon, sweetie," Erin told him, bending to clean up a few crayons that had been knocked to the floor.

As she straightened, a tear dropped to the desk in front

of the boy. He quickly wiped at his cheeks and turned away from her.

Isaac had been a tough nut to crack. He rarely interacted with the other kids and usually stayed in the corner pretending to read a book that was far above his basic reading level or doing a puzzle. She'd talked to his classroom teacher and the school counselor, but both women had seemed at a loss for how to reach him. Phone calls to Joel and his mother, Danielle, had gone unanswered and voice mails not returned. Both mom and dad shut Erin down when she tried to speak to them at pickup.

It sometimes felt like the only emotion the boy could access was anger, so to see him embarrassed by his tears broke her heart.

"Do you want to talk about it?" she asked softly, resting her hip on the desk across from where he sat.

He shook his head and refused to meet her gaze.

"Fritzi and Otis were really cool. I noticed Otis seemed to like you a lot." What Erin had witnessed was Isaac planting himself at the dog's side and refusing to give up his spot. He'd spent the entire visit gently stroking Otis's furry head and bending down to whisper in his ear. Thanks to his training as a therapy dog, Otis had been patient with the attention. The other kids had seemed to take it as Isaac's due that he got the prime real estate to love on the animal.

"My dad gave away Jack," he whispered, his voice cracking on the last word.

"Was Jack your dog?"

Isaac looked up, tears shining in his eyes. "The best dog ever. But sometimes he got scared when dad yelled and it made him pee on the floor."

"Some dogs get nervous with loud noises," Erin agreed. Like Caden, Isaac rarely spoke more than monosyllabic responses to the direct questions she asked. It both thrilled her and hurt her heart that he was sharing this small piece of his life with her now.

"He barked, too, but never at me. He loved me best of all."

She fisted her hands at her side, every part of her wanting to reach out and hug the boy but afraid of scaring him away if she did. "I can understand why. You were great with Otis."

"We'll get another dog," a soft voice said from behind Erin.

She whirled around to see Isaac's mother standing in the doorway, not bothering to wipe away the tears that stained her cheeks. Danielle Rodriguez was petite, with beautiful dark hair that fell to the middle of her back and wide-set eyes. Erin guessed they were about the same age, although Danielle's features had a weariness and worldliness stamped across them that came from too many years of hard work, hard living and struggling to raise three kids on her own.

"Your father is not living in my house anymore," she said, switching her gaze to Erin, then back to her son. "And that two-timing jerk isn't invited back. We'll start looking for a dog when I get off work tomorrow. I promise."

Isaac was out of his chair in an instant, hurtling toward his mother and wrapping his arms tight around her waist.

She bent to hug him close, and a lump formed in Erin's throat at the tenderness of the moment. Maybe her program was having the impact she'd hoped for after all.

After a few minutes, Danielle straightened. "Get your backpack and lunch box, Isaac," she told her son, dropping a kiss on the top of his head. "Your sister has dinner going at home." Isaac moved toward the row of backpacks, and

Danielle turned to Erin. "I know Joel sees this program as a way to get out of spending time with him on the days when I work late."

Erin acknowledged that truth with a small nod. "Whatever the reason, I'm glad he's here."

"Me, too," Danielle said, squaring her shoulders. "We've got a long way to go, but kicking Joel to the curb was a good start."

"Will he still be a part of Isaac's life?"

Danielle shrugged. "If he gets his act together. My boy wants his father in his life. But I'm done with Joel, and he's mad as hell. Thinks being my baby daddy gives him a right to whatever he wants from me. He's a cheater and a liar. I deserve better than that."

"You do," Erin agreed instantly.

Isaac came over with his backpack. Although the scowl was back on his face, his little shoulders seemed to carry less of a weight than they did minutes earlier.

"We're going to get another dog," he said quietly, leaning in close to his mother and glancing up at Erin.

"I promise," Danielle whispered, ruffling his hair.

"I'll text you Caden Sharpe's number," Erin told her. "He's the man who brought the therapy pets to visit us today. He runs a small rescue organization out of one of the barns on his ranch. Maybe he can help you find a new dog."

"Thank you," Danielle said. "For everything."

Erin nodded and spent another twenty minutes cleaning up and preparing for Friday's class. She trimmed the stems of the flowers David had given her and put them in a vase before leaving the community center. Most nights classes ran past the time she finished, so there was always someone at the reception desk.

She waved goodbye and walked out into the darkening

night. The crisp breeze made her pull in a sharp breath. The change of seasons was a fickle time in Crimson. Summer could linger for weeks, then disappear within a day. Sometimes fall would last just as long, but more often winter inserted an icy blast of cold to remind everyone what to expect over the next several months.

Colder weather made Erin wish for things she didn't have, like someone to cuddle up to on a frosty winter night. Sugar was a great cat, but not much of a snuggler. It was time to put the heavier comforter on her bed and get out her cold-weather clothes. Maybe she needed to give Caden a call and adopt another furry friend.

She knocked her closed fist against her forehead several times to stop pathetic internal ramblings. In her mind, she'd already skimmed past the date with David to when he inevitably lost interest in her. She'd become one of those single women whose only emotionally intimate relationships were with her pets.

"I don't know what you're thinking," a voice said from the shadows, "but I like that head of yours way too much to watch you abuse it."

She looked up to see David standing a few feet away, hands shoved deep in the front pockets of his jeans. He'd put a heavy canvas jacket on over the flannel shirt he'd worn earlier to pick up Rhett. The bulk of it made him look even broader than normal.

His hair was, as usual, casually tousled, and a hint of stubble shadowed his jaw. He was every one of Erin's fantasies come to life, and it positively terrified her.

"Silly thoughts," she mumbled. "What are you doing here? Is everything okay with Rhett?"

"He's fine. The bar is slow tonight so I had Tracie come up to stay with him and my mom for a few minutes." He took a step closer. "I wanted to see you."

"Hi," she whispered as he drew her forward, wrapping his arms around her. She shivered as he nuzzled his nose against her throat. "You're cold."

"I was waiting for you to keep me warm," he said into her skin, and it was like he'd read her mind.

"Thank you again for the flowers," she said, then lifted onto her toes and kissed him. It was the first time she'd initiated a kiss, and he seemed happy to let her take the lead.

Despite the chilly air, Erin's whole body ignited in flames. She was so lost to this man. While it might be her downfall, she couldn't bring herself to care.

"Tell me about Caden Sharpe," he said when she finally pulled back.

It was difficult to remember her own name, let alone anything else, so it took Erin a few moments to answer. "He's a way nicer guy than people give him credit for. I think he's just misunderstood because of his past and the trouble he got into as a kid."

He studied her face as if trying to decipher some sort of complicated puzzle, which was crazy because Erin had always been an open book.

"Do you always see the best in people?" he asked finally.

"I try to. Is that a bad thing?"

"No. It's one of the things I—" He coughed and cleared his throat. "One of the things that makes you special. You realize Sharpe likes you."

"Because he was kind enough to bring a couple of therapy pets to visit the kids?" She rolled her eyes. "He was doing a favor for a friend and I benefited from it."

"I saw how he looked at you and—"

"Are you jealous?" Erin felt her mouth drop open. "Oh my gosh, I got flowers and a man is jealous over me. Those are two firsts in one day." She pulled away and did a little two-step dance routine in front of him.

"I'm not jealous," David muttered through his teeth. "But don't go out with him, okay?"

She stopped dancing and moved closer. "Of course I'm not going to go out with him. I'm going on a date with you."

He blinked several times. "Some women date more than one man at a time."

"I'm not one of those," she assured him, then wound her arms around his neck and kissed him again. She knew her reaction made her seem like the biggest dork in the world, but she didn't care. This man, who made her heart sing, had brought her flowers *and* wanted her for himself. "I only want you. But I'm flattered that you're jealous."

"Flattered?" He gave a small laugh. "You should tell me to mind my own damn business."

"I like being your business, as long as you know I'm going to continue to see Caden. He and the animals help with the kids."

He inclined his head. "I'd never tell you who you can or can't see. I just want to be sure *you* know you're mine."

Erin's mouth went dry. She'd never had anyone claim her before, and the thought of it was both exhilarating and terrifying.

Then a movement behind David distracted her. A man with a dark hoodie seemed to be watching them from the shadows of the nearby alley. "Um, okay… I think."

David looked over his shoulder, following her gaze, and the man quickly walked down the street away from them.

"Did you know him?" David asked gently.

"I don't think so."

"Where's your car?"

"It's fine," she assured him. "This is Crimson."

"Humor me," he insisted. He kissed the tip of her nose, then walked her to her car.

After a few more kisses, she drove home, tingling from the ends of her hair to her toes. She'd been *claimed* and could barely wait to see what that meant for Saturday.

Chapter Twelve

An unfamiliar lightness bubbled up in David at the sight of Erin waiting for him outside her apartment building Saturday morning. It was as if he'd taken a big swig of champagne and the bubbles were rioting around his stomach. His feelings for her were different from anything he'd experienced before. Today was his chance to make her understand how much she meant to him.

But he had no plan to blurt out that he loved her, as he'd almost done when she was in his arms. Hell, he'd known her for only a few weeks and he wasn't built for love in the first place.

Longing was a different story. The yearning he felt for her pulsed through him like blood in his veins. She gave him hope and made him happy in a way he hadn't even thought possible.

It had seemed like a joke when she'd asked him for an affair. Physical desire was one thing, but his need for

Erin transcended what his body wanted. In such a short time she'd become like the air he breathed, necessary for his very survival.

So he had to make this day count.

As soon as he pulled to a stop, she opened the truck's passenger-side door and climbed in.

"I'm ready for our adventure," she said, tossing her tote bag into the back seat.

He grinned and flipped his sunglasses onto his forehead. "I can see that. You know, I would have come to pick you up at your door." He reached into the back seat and handed her another bouquet of flowers. "I brought these for you."

Color rushed into her cheeks as she gazed at them. "I must seem like a total fool," she said, biting down on her lip. "I know the woman is supposed to wait for the man, but I was so excited and it's a gorgeous day and—"

He leaned in and kissed her, breathing in to capture her scent and the sweetness that always seemed to surround her. "I've been watching the clock all morning," he admitted. "I couldn't wait for this date to begin."

"Let me run and put these in water." She opened the door, then looked back at him over her shoulder. "You don't have to bring me flowers."

"I'm courting you," he reminded her.

She flashed a shy smile. "I don't think I've ever been courted before."

"It's a first for me, too."

"You're doing pretty darn well," she said, and hopped out of the truck.

His cell phone rang as he watched her enter the building. Pulling it out of his pocket, he said a silent prayer everything was okay with Rhett. His nephew had been invited to a birthday party for one of his friends from school, and David's mother had promised she'd get him there safely and follow all the house rules David had set.

He'd asked Tracie, who was working all day, to keep an eye on them this morning. Later this afternoon, David's friend Jase Crenshaw, who had a stepson only a year older than Rhett, was going to take the boys to the park and out for ice cream. He'd also asked Olivia Travers to stop by, trying to cover all his bases to make sure Rhett was safe.

Angela seemed to take it all in stride. Since the fiasco on the mountain, she'd been on her best behavior and David had to admit he was grateful to his mother for her help.

It wasn't a local number flashing on his screen, and he recognized the Phoenix area code from where Jenna was doing her stint in rehab. His stomach in knots, he accepted the call, only to have his sister immediately lay into him.

"I can't believe you're messing around with Rhett's teacher," she said, her voice a low hiss.

"Jenna," he said, breathing out a sigh. "Is everything okay?"

"Do I sound okay? I had to trade three packs of Skittles to be able to make this phone call. You know how I love Skittles."

One side of his mouth curved. "I know. Exactly why are you calling?"

"To tell you to leave Ms. MacDonald alone."

"How do you even—"

"Mom told me. She said you've got the hots for Rhett's teacher and you're even taking her out on a date. As far as I know, you haven't dated anyone since you moved to Crimson and you can't start with the teacher. She's off-limits."

"Why?" he asked, trying to keep his temper under wraps. His sister was doing great in her program, but he knew she was still fragile. The last thing he needed was to set her off.

She blew an agitated breath into the phone. "Rhett loves that woman and whatever program of hers he's going to in the afternoons. It's all he talks about when he calls."

"She's great with him."

"Yeah, so if you piss her off by treating her like crap, she could take it out on him."

"She'd never do that," he answered automatically, then added, "Besides, I'm not going to hurt her."

"You hurt everybody."

The words were like a knife to his gut, because coming from his sister they meant so much more. Unwanted memories flooded through him. He swallowed against the bile rising in his throat, trying to forget. Willing himself to forget.

"I know I've messed things up royally," Jenna said in a quieter tone, "and I appreciate you stepping in to help with Rhett. I need his world to be stable, David. I need to believe he's going to get through this. She's a big part of that."

So am I, he wanted to argue, but only repeated, "I'm not going to hurt her."

At that moment Erin emerged from the apartment building, smiling as she walked toward him. If his sister was right, he should throw the truck into Reverse and drive away before this went any further. Because there was no doubt in his mind how far he'd take it if Erin got in next to him.

All the way.

"Promise me you'll leave her alone," his sister whispered.

"I've got to go," he said as an answer. "You take care of you, Jenna. I've got things under control."

He ended the call before she could argue, and he had no doubt she would if given the chance. His sister had seen him at his worst, just like he had with her. How could either of them believe the other had things under control?

Erin climbed into the truck. "I'm ready." She turned to him and her smile disappeared. "What's wrong? I saw you on the phone. Is it Rhett?"

"My sister called." He tapped his fingers on the steering wheel, wishing he hadn't talked to Jenna. All of his happiness from earlier had been colored by her doubts, which mingled with his into some sort of poison that seeped into every cell.

Erin placed a hand on his arm, and the gentle touch felt like a brand through the fabric of his shirt. "Is she okay?"

"She told me not to go out with you," he said quietly. As much as he didn't want to share Jenna's warning with Erin, it was the only way through this.

"She doesn't even know me." Erin drew back her hand. "Is it the mercy date thing?"

He shifted to face her. "What 'mercy date thing'?"

"You taking me out as a thank-you for helping with Rhett." She made a face. "Because of that stupid comment I made about the affair."

David raked a hand through his hair. He hated the doubt that now shadowed Erin's dark eyes. He'd done his best to plan a perfect day, and now it was tainted before they even started.

"She doesn't want me to go out with you because you're too good for me. She thinks I'm going to hurt you."

When Erin didn't immediately refute his sister's claim, David slammed a hand against the steering wheel. "Damn it," he muttered. "You agree. We haven't even started and you think I'm going to hurt you."

He stared out the front of the truck, unable to look at

her and see the truth on her face. This was his chance. *She* was his chance to finally get something wholly right in his life. And not one person believed he could do it.

"David."

"We should end this now," he told her. "I don't want to hurt you."

"There are no guarantees in life." He felt her press closer. "Please look at me."

He gave a small laugh, then turned. "I can't resist a 'please,' either." Her face was only inches away from his and, once again, her beauty slayed him. He focused on the tiny flecks of gold at the edges of her dark eyes and tried not to think about losing her before she was even his.

"My life has been safe for as long as I can remember. I didn't risk anything and had little to lose. My job is stable, my boyfriend bored me to tears. Typically, the most excitement I have is when a new book from one of my favorite authors comes out."

He smiled. "I'm going to read one of those romance novels so I know what all the hype is about."

She rolled her eyes. "My point is that with you, I feel like I'm living the adventure I've always wanted."

"You're doing that on your own," he countered. "You're helping with Rhett. You've made a difference in the lives of the kids in your program. It's you, Erin."

"Then I'm happy to share it with you." She sat back and arched a brow at him. "You know, I could be the one to hurt you. I could break your heart."

David opened his mouth to tell her his heart was too closed off to be in any danger of breaking. But at that moment a flash of pain pierced his chest so sharply it made his breath catch. "Anything is possible," he answered instead, struggling to keep his voice neutral.

"That's right," she agreed, thankfully oblivious to the

strange things going on inside him. "Anything is possible. Life is a gamble. I want to take a risk with you, David. No matter what the outcome."

Despite his reckless youth, all his life, David had made decisions based on keeping himself or the people in his life safe. Baseball gave him a way out of his tumultuous childhood. Moving to Crimson had made it easier to watch out for Jenna and Rhett. The brewery gave him a stable income doing something he was good at. He'd always chosen women who wanted nothing more from him than a good time. Being with Erin wasn't safe—for either of them.

But she was worth the risk.

He leaned in and kissed her deeply, realizing he'd quickly become addicted to the taste of her. The more time he spent with her, the more he wanted.

How could he consider pushing her away? She was too important, and he wasn't going to hurt her. He wouldn't let himself.

"Are you ready for the best day of your life?" he asked, finally pulling back and shifting the truck into gear.

She laughed. "Pretty confident in yourself."

"I'm confident in us," he corrected and turned the truck toward the highway.

Butterflies danced through Erin's stomach as David drove out of town. It had been easy enough to toss off the comment about either of them getting hurt, but she had no doubt her heart was on the line.

As much as she'd tried to stop her feelings from spiraling out of control, Erin was falling for this man. Hard. If this day was half as good as he promised, she'd be a goner for sure.

But she hadn't been lying when she told him he was worth the risk. Her life had been spent taking the safe path, but the only things that had gotten her were frustration and discontent.

Even if she lost her heart, at least she could say she tried.

They headed up the mountain, and he turned off at the sign for Cloud Cabin.

"This is private land," she said, even as she leaned forward to gaze up at the tall pines arching over the road.

"I know," he answered.

"Crimson Ranch owns Cloud Cabin. Josh and Sara opened it last year for their guests. I guess a lot of family reunions and corporate events are held there in the summer."

One side of his mouth crooked. "Yep."

She figured David must know what he was doing, but curiosity niggled at her. "Are we trespassing?"

"Nope."

"Are you going to tell me anything?"

"You look beautiful."

Erin sat back in her seat and didn't bother to hide her smile. Even if David had doubts and his sister had doubts and everyone around them had doubts, this day felt perfect to Erin. "It's an adventure," she whispered.

A couple of miles in, a driveway split off to the right. David took the turn and within a few minutes they arrived at Cloud Cabin. The house was magnificent, large without being ostentatious and made completely out of hewn logs. A patio wrapped around two sides of the cabin on the second floor, and she could see a fire pit and several pieces of outdoor furniture arranged at the far end.

"It's amazing," she whispered.

David parked the car in front of one of the three garage bays on the lower level. "Some famous architect Sara knows designed it. They brought in the timber from Montana, but sourced the rock locally from the quarry near Meeker."

"What's that?" She pointed to the small cabin that sat at the other side of the clearing.

"Caretaker's cabin," David told her. "When they have big groups at Cloud Cabin, the staff stays there."

"Is anyone up here now?"

"You and me." He bussed her cheek.

She found herself unable to move even as he got out of the truck and came around to open her door.

"You okay, honey?"

She bit down on her lip. "I've lived in this town most of my life, so I'm used to seeing rich people. I've had wealthy students and walked the streets of Aspen, but I've never… I've never actually been in a place like this."

He leaned in and whispered in her ear, "You have to get out of the truck if you're going to make it to the cabin today."

She laughed and pushed him away. "You make fun, but that's because you were a rich and famous baseball player. You probably hung out on yachts and stuff."

"A few speedboats in Miami, but no yachts." He took her hand and tugged until she stepped out onto the gravel driveway. "Money makes things easier, but it's not important beyond that."

"What people do with it is important," she corrected. "Like fund an after-school program."

"And that," he agreed. "This place is ours for the day. Let's go explore it."

He laced his fingers with hers as they walked up the flagstone path that led to the front door. David produced a key from his pocket and unlocked the door, holding it open for Erin to walk in.

She wasn't sure what she expected, but it wasn't a space

that immediately seemed to wrap around her and make her feel at home. The foyer was cozy and bright, with framed paintings of mountain vistas on each wall. The family room was situated to one side. Rich, colorful rugs covered the hardwood floor, and overstuffed furniture had been arranged to make a cozy sitting area in front of the massive stone fireplace.

"What do you want to do first?" he asked. "There are ATVs in the garage, a hot tub out back." He led her into the kitchen, where wood cabinets and gorgeous marble countertops balanced the industrial feel of gleaming stainless steel appliances.

"I could make us something to eat."

She glanced up at him. "You're going to cook?"

"Let me rephrase that," he said. "I could heat up the food that the head chef at the brewery prepared for us."

She grinned. "You've thought of everything."

He turned to her fully, wrapped his arms around her waist. "I wanted this day to be about you and me. No distractions. No real life butting its ugly head in. You and me."

"You and me," she repeated, and held on tight as he claimed her mouth. It was like they were the only two people in the world, and she let all her worries and doubts drift away. He lifted her into his arms, then sat her on the edge of the counter, pressing himself into the V of her legs.

Her body tingled with need and awareness, and she could feel that he wanted her, too. It made her want to forget everything else and beg him to take her to the bedroom. What would it be like to spend an entire day in bed with this man?

The air seemed to get caught in her throat at the thought, because what if she ruined everything by not knowing what she was doing. Kissing was one thing, but the rest…

"ATVs," she blurted, wrenching herself away from him.

He stared at her as if she were speaking a foreign language, then laughed softly. "ATVs it is."

Chapter Thirteen

David breathed in the pine-scented air and tried to keep his focus on the path in front of him, and not on Erin's body pressed tight against his on the back of the ATV.

Once again, his desire for her had almost gotten the best of him. If she hadn't stopped it, he would have taken her right on the counter…or the floor…or wherever she would have him. He'd arranged with Josh to borrow the cabin so he could give Erin a day away from the responsibilities of life but still remain close to town if Rhett needed him.

It was becoming more and more difficult to keep his mind on anything except what she would feel like under him and how much he wanted to explore every inch of her beautiful body.

She shifted behind him, and he slowed the powerful machine, not wanting to scare her. Instead, she leaned in closer and shouted, "Faster." That was all the encouragement David needed to hit the throttle.

He tightened his grip on the ATV's handles and maneuvered through the pine forest and out into a clearing that overlooked the valley below them. As soon as he pulled to a stop and cut the motor, Erin jumped off the back.

"That was so cool," she cried, bouncing up and down on her toes. "We were flying."

He grinned at her happiness. Everything with Erin felt new and made him want to shake off his typical attitude and see the world through her eyes.

"Can I drive on the way back?"

"Of course." He gestured to the meadow behind them. "The trail loops around this field. You can use it like a practice course."

"On my own?" she asked, her eyes bright with excitement.

He laughed. "Ditching me already? Yes, I brought picnic supplies. I'll lay everything out while you take this baby for a ride."

He unloaded the soft-sided cooler and blanket he'd packed in the ATV's cargo area. Despite the fact that it was early October, they'd been blessed with a summer-like day. The sun shone brightly in the clear blue sky, and even the breeze that whispered through the trees felt warm.

"Climb on," he told her, then stifled a groan at the way her eyes widened. "The ATV," he clarified, wishing he'd locked her in the cabin and had his wicked way with her when he had the chance.

Instead he watched her position herself on the ATV. He gave instructions on how to put it into gear, braking and steering around turns. Erin's fingers trembled slightly as she gripped the handlebars. He wrapped his hand around hers. "Don't be nervous."

"I've never even driven a stick shift," she admitted.

"We'll put that on the list," he assured her, "and this is way easier. Just don't make sharp turns going fast."

"Because I'll flip it?" she asked, biting down on her lip.

He couldn't resist the urge to brush a quick kiss across her mouth. "You're not going to flip it. Go get 'em, Erin Earnhardt."

She turned the key, then shifted the machine into gear. He gave her a thumbs-up when she glanced over at him, and with a nod she hit the gas and took off down the path.

The ATV lurched forward several times as she got used to driving it. But after a few minutes, she was moving at a steady pace around the perimeter of the meadow. Slow but steady.

She pulled to a stop in front of him when she'd circled the entire path and clapped her hands together. "How'd I do?"

"Great. But you can go a little faster if you want."

She scrunched up her nose. "That was boring, right?"

"Watching you is never boring, but trust yourself. You can handle the machine." He reached out and tugged on the end of her ponytail. "You can handle anything."

Determination seeped into her gaze, lighting her eyes with a fire that made him want to shout for joy. This was the woman he knew and…

Once again, not going there.

She steered the ATV down the path once more. Within minutes, David regretted his words as the ATV went faster and faster around the dirt trail. He motioned for her to slow down as she sped past him, but she either didn't see or chose to ignore the warning. Her hair came undone and flew out behind her, like she was some ancient Amazon warrior racing into battle.

He held his breath as the ATV suddenly veered sharply to the right, and two of the wheels lifted from the ground.

"No," he shouted, already running toward her.

At the last second, Erin shifted her weight and the machine straightened on the path once more.

David bent forward, placing his palms on his knees as he struggled to pull air in and out of his lungs. The ATV was at his side a moment later, and he quickly turned the key, then hauled her into his arms.

"What the hell happened?" He hugged her close, then gripped the sides of her head with his hands, moving her away enough that he could examine her face. "Are you okay?"

She grinned up at him. "Did you see me go up on two wheels?"

"See you," he shouted. "I almost had a heart attack watching you. I thought I said no sharp turns."

"A chipmunk ran across the trail."

He couldn't understand how she remained so calm when his heart was rioting in his chest. "I didn't want to hurt him."

"So flipping the machine seemed like a better alternative?"

She laughed and smoothed the hair from his forehead. "I didn't flip. I had the whole thing under control. Remember, I can handle anything."

He stared at her for a moment, taking in the pure joy on her face. "You're really okay?"

"Maybe your mom was onto something when she said you were a worrywart."

"My mom has no idea what she's talking about."

Erin reached up and covered his hands with hers, a frown pulling on the corners of her mouth. "You're shaking," she whispered.

"You scared the hell out of me." He closed his eyes

and leaned in to place a kiss on her forehead. "Adventure is fun, but it would kill me if I couldn't keep you safe."

He touched his lips to each of her eyelids, then trailed kisses down her cheek and along her jawline. It was as if he needed to touch every part of her to reassure himself she was okay.

"I'm fine," she assured him. "I'm sorry I scared you." She tilted her head so that her mouth met his, and the kiss quickly turned molten. He couldn't wait anymore. His body still shook from fear of her being hurt, and he channeled his thundering emotions into the kiss. Scooping her into his arms, he strode across the field to the place he'd spread out the blanket and lowered her to it.

The sun remained warm on his back and he buried his nose in the crook of Erin's neck, breathing in her scent mixed with the smell of pine trees and fresh mountain air. It was intoxicating in a way not even the finest liquor or the most powerful drug could be, and he was an instant addict.

His body trembled as he tried to control his need, to take things slow, to allow this to be her choice. More than anything, he wanted her to choose him.

"I want you," she whispered into his ear, and it was like every prayer he'd never had the guts to say had been answered.

For a moment Erin wondered if she'd said the wrong thing. David stilled above her, the muscles of his back going rigid under her hands.

He lifted his head, the intensity in his blue eyes stoking the fire inside her almost as much as his kisses had.

"I had a plan for this," he told her, his voice rough. "Champagne and rose petals and—"

"Actual rose petals?" she asked on a hoarse laugh.

To her surprise, pink tinged his cheeks. Who knew she could make David McCay blush?

"It seemed like something one of your romance heroes would do," he told her.

"You're the only man I want." She ran her hands down his back and up under the hem of his sweater. He gritted his teeth as she drew her nails along the bare skin of his back. "And I've waited long enough, David. Please don't make me wait anymore."

"I guess I can't refuse since you said please," he whispered against her lips.

Then he kissed her again and all her senses began to sing, a choir of desire and lust building in her body. After a few minutes he sat back, straddling her legs as he knelt. He slowly unbuttoned her denim shirt, his gaze fierce as inch by inch, her skin was revealed to him.

She shrugged the shirt off her shoulders, any wariness she had about being with a man so much more experienced than she was forgotten because of the longing reflected in his eyes. Longing for her.

The sun was like a warm bath on her skin, and she reached forward and tugged his sweater up and over his head.

She'd seen his chest before, but the sunlight casting his body in silhouette was perfection. He rolled to one side and quickly toed off his boots and undid his jeans, pushing them down over his lean hips.

Reaching behind her back, she unhooked the clasp of her bra and let the soft satin material fall away from her body, then shimmied out of her jeans and panties. David let out a small groan as he knelt at her side again, a condom packet held between two fingers.

"You make me want to lose myself," he said, covering

her body with his. "You make me forget everything except this moment."

"I think that's the point," she said, then gasped as he filled her. She wound her arms around his neck and kissed him, arching up so that every part of her touched every part of him.

He groaned in response and she felt an unfamiliar surge of power lick through her. She could feel that he was holding himself back, trying to take it slow because that's what a woman like Erin would want. But she wanted *more*. She wanted everything, and David was the man she wanted to give it to her.

Or even better, she'd take it from him. She moved her hips at the same time she raked her nails over his muscled shoulders. "Let go," she whispered, and without even having to add "please," he gave her exactly what she wanted.

They found a rhythm all their own, deep and intense and exactly what Erin craved. Her pleasure built in thick waves and she lost herself in the sensation of it and the fact that David seemed as overwhelmed by desire as she felt. He whispered her name like a prayer and buried his face in her neck. Then he nipped at the sensitive flesh of her ear and Erin spun out of control, gripping him tighter as she hurtled over the edge of passion.

He followed a moment later and Erin wasn't sure if it was her own heartbeat or his she heard pounding through her head. He continued to kiss her throat as she came back down, humming soothing little sounds against her skin.

"That was incredible," David whispered into her hair. "You were incredible."

Erin still felt like she was floating through the air, and the only thing that tethered her to earth was his deep voice. It was as if she'd shrugged off the old, boring version of herself and had begun to step into becoming the person she was meant to be.

"*We* were incredible," she corrected him, because she knew that nothing in her life would ever compare to this moment. Whether they lasted another week or for an eternity—and how she longed for an eternity—he would always hold her heart.

Even though he hadn't said the words *I love you*, she had to believe he felt something for her. It was in the way he looked at her, the intensity of his touch, the way her body came alive as he moved inside her.

"Are you hungry?" He trailed his fingers over her stomach in small figure-eight patterns. "You distracted me with your race car ATV driving and I never got the food unpacked."

She kissed his shoulder. "I think you distracted me by getting naked," she said, earning a rumbling laugh from him. "But now I'm starving."

After several long, lingering kisses, he rolled away from her and she grabbed her clothes. As she dressed, Erin looked around in wonder. She'd just had the most amazing sex she could ever imagine in the woods. Outside. She almost giggled at the thought of it. Talk about an adventure.

They ate the lunch he'd packed, sandwiches, fresh fruit and the best chocolate chip cookies she'd ever tasted. After repacking everything into the ATV, they took a short hike up to another overlook. Erin told him more about her relationship with her mother and her friends at school. While David peppered her with questions, he offered little about his life in return.

"What happened to Jenna?" she asked finally, as they stood together gazing out over the valley.

"You were there that night," he said casually. "You saw her apartment and—"

"I'm not talking about recently." She made her voice level, even though nerves tumbled through her. "I mean years ago. Something happened, and I don't know what it was, but it's clear you feel responsible for it."

He dropped her hand and stalked toward the path that led to the ATV. For a moment she thought he was going to leave her standing by herself in the woods. How was it possible he'd willingly shared his body with her but not whatever it was that so obviously burdened him about his sister?

Just before disappearing around the bend, he turned and walked back to her, his gaze fierce.

"I've never talked to anyone about Jenna," he said.

"Let me be the first."

He was silent for so long she thought he might refuse. Then he gave a jerky nod. "I started playing for a club baseball team in high school. Kids from the area, but no one from my neighborhood. These were boys whose parents could afford to sponsor the team, buy us the best equipment and make sure college scouts took notice. I knew my only chance of getting out of our crappy neighborhood was a scholarship." He shook his head. "Jenna didn't like the team because it took me away from home. We were on the road a lot during the summer."

"It was your dream," Erin said softly.

"Yeah," he agreed, his voice filled with bitterness. "My dream. Mom had started dating a new guy around that time and it got serious real quick. I didn't mind the guy—he wasn't as bad as some of her boyfriends—but Jenna didn't like him. He got too into the 'father' role, trying to impose house rules and curfews."

"This man lived with your family?"

David shrugged. "Not officially, but he stayed over a lot. Mom definitely knew how to pick the losers. Jenna asked me to kick him out or talk to Mom about kicking him out, but I was too busy with baseball to even care. The dude left me alone. It was Jenna he wanted to fall into line. Her wild streak had always been blatant and she was mouthy with anyone who gave her grief about it."

"She sounds like a lot to handle."

"We mostly raised ourselves, so she wasn't much into being 'handled.'" He gave a small laugh. "She still isn't. But it doesn't excuse what happened to her."

His shoulders rose and fell, as if he was struggling to catch his breath. Suddenly all of it came together. His protective instinct around his sister while holding tight to the belief that he'd failed her. The ambivalence toward his mother. Her mouth went dry but she forced out the words, "Did your mother's boyfriend—"

"He tried but Jenna fought him off." His hands fisted at his sides. "He knocked her around pretty good, but my mom came home from work. He went after her, too, but a neighbor called the cops and he was arrested." He turned to her, his eyes bleak. "I should have been home that day after school. We didn't even have baseball practice, but some of the guys were hanging out so I went with them instead."

She grabbed his hand and forced open his fist, lacing her fingers with his. "It wasn't your fault, David. You were a teenage boy. How were you supposed to know something like that would happen?"

"Jenna asked me to walk home with her," he whispered. "She didn't like being alone in the apartment with Mom's boyfriends. I told her she'd watched too many after-school movies and she was just trying to get attention." He blew out a breath. "She never forgave me."

Erin moved so she stood directly in front of him and waited until he finally looked down at her.

"She hasn't forgiven you? Or you haven't forgiven yourself?"

Chapter Fourteen

David stared down into Erin's luminous brown eyes, unable to speak. To his knowledge, Jenna and their mother were the only people in the world who knew about what had happened that afternoon. They were the only ones who truly understood how badly he'd failed them.

Until now.

He'd been reluctant to share the memory with Erin, terrified it would change things between them. How could she not despise him after how much his selfish choice had cost his family?

But instead of judgment, her gaze was filled with sympathy and…could that possibly be understanding he saw when she looked at him?

"What's the difference?" he asked when he finally found his voice. "I failed her. I failed my mother."

"Your mother's boyfriend was at fault. You were a kid."

"I was the man of the house," he insisted, because that

was the truth he knew. A tear spilled from the corner of her eye, and he caught it with his thumb. "Why are you crying? The last thing I want to do is make you cry."

She gently pushed at his chest, but when he started to take a step back, she leaned in and wrapped her arms around his waist. "You big oaf," she said into his jacket. "I'm crying *for* you. For all the years you've carried that guilt around inside you and punished yourself for something that was *not* your fault."

Her words stunned him. He'd never cared about anyone's opinion of him. David made his own luck in life—good or bad—and he told himself that's how he liked it. But something unfurled in his chest as he held Erin, looking out to the town that had become his true home. She still wanted him despite his failures, and the realization made him almost dizzy with relief.

"Don't cry, sweetheart," he whispered, resting his chin on the top of her head and rubbing her back. "I'm not worth a single one of your tears."

"You are," she insisted, sniffing loudly. "You're worth a lot more than you believe. I hate that you can't see the man that I do when I look at you."

He closed his eyes and breathed in the scent of her, let it wash away all the bad things he believed about himself—if only for a short time. Hell, it was good to feel truly happy. "I think that makes us even," he told her, "because I hate that you think you're ordinary."

She gave a soft laugh and wiped her face on his jacket. "That's different."

He tipped up her face and kissed her. "You are beautiful, extraordinary and special to me."

Her lips curved into a smile against his. "This is the best date ever."

"And we haven't even hit the hot tub," he said, earning another laugh.

Feeling lighter than he had in years, David led her back down the trail to the ATV. He insisted she drive back to the cabin, a fact he was pretty certain thrilled her given how many times she let out whoops of delight as she maneuvered through the trees.

They changed into bathing suits kept at the cabin for guests, and he opened a bottle of wine before climbing into the bubbling hot tub with a breathtaking view of the surrounding peaks.

The wine lasted longer than the bathing suits, and it wasn't long before he carried Erin into the cabin's master bedroom and made love to her again.

He'd assumed being with her would make the pounding need inside him lessen, but every touch and whisper that crossed her lips only made him want her more. There had never been anyone like her in his life. For the first time ever, he wanted to claim a woman as his and never let go.

The sun dipped over the mountain far too soon and they made their way back down to town.

He'd called both his mother and Tracie from the cabin's landline to check on Rhett and how the day was going. The boy had been thrilled with all the attention he was getting during the day, but when he heard his uncle was with Erin, he begged David to bring her home to have dinner with them.

"Is your mother going to be okay with that?" Erin took his hand as they drove down the mountain road.

"My guess is she'd rather have you there than me," he told her.

"That's not true. She loves you." Erin squeezed his fingers. "She's your mother, David."

"Right. And when do I get to meet your mom?"

Immediately she tried to pull her hand away from his, but he quickly interlaced their fingers.

"My mom and dad wouldn't believe we're together," she told him.

He felt embarrassment wash through him and struggled to keep his voice even. "Because I didn't graduate from college?"

"No," she insisted. "Not at all. You're a former baseball star and you own the hottest bar in Crimson. She's even been to Elevation. My mom likes the honey wheat beer and the artichoke dip."

"It's a real crowd pleaser, but I think you've got it all wrong. I could throw a ball and now I make beer. It's not the same as what you do, Erin. You change kids' lives."

"Kindergarten is just colors and shapes and noise control according to her."

"It's a big deal," David told her, willing her to believe him. To recognize how amazing she was and all she'd accomplished. "How long have you been a teacher?"

"Seven years."

"So your first class of students is in sixth grade?"

She nodded. "Their last year at the elementary school before junior high."

"I bet more than a few of them still visit you."

"Of course. They come in at recess or help me during my planning session."

"Do they do that for all the teachers?"

He studied her face as he waited for an answer. He could see her mulling over the question and how to respond. "It's just that I'm the most accessible," she said finally.

"Crimson Elementary is one building. All the teachers are accessible. You make an impression, Erin. How many famous people have you heard refer to teachers who made a difference in their lives?"

She rolled her eyes. "They're talking about college professors like my father was or acting teachers or vocal coaches. Not kindergarten."

"You're making a difference to Rhett."

"Because he's a great kid."

"Jase Crenshaw told me his stepson with Asperger's still asks for you to be his teacher."

"Davey is really special, too."

"Which kids aren't special to you?"

He turned down the alley behind Elevation and parked in his spot in back of the kitchen.

"They're all special," she answered immediately.

"You have to admit some of them are little pains in the neck. I know I was." He turned off the ignition and braced himself for her response.

"Don't say that. I'm sure you were adorable at five."

"I was a hellion."

"The kids I have are amazing."

"What about Isaac Martin?"

She hesitated, then said, "Well, I never had him as a student because they moved to Crimson last year. But I've been getting to know him in the after-school program and he's actually quite sensitive. I think the trouble between his parents caused him to act out, but his mom changing things around will help."

"You proved my point." He hopped out of the truck and walked around to her door. When she climbed out, he took her hand. "You're the kind of teacher who believes in the potential of each of her kids."

"Kindergarten is all about potential."

"Tapping into that potential is all about you."

She opened her mouth, as if to argue with him, then

snapped it shut. Her eyes widened and a smile lit up her entire face. "I'm good at what I do," she said softly, as if it were a new revelation to her. "I'm really good."

"The best," he agreed. "Don't let anyone make you feel like you don't matter. You do."

They walked through the narrow space between the buildings, and David unlocked the door leading up to the apartment.

"This day was perfect." Erin leaned in to kiss him.

"You're perfect," he said. And for the first time in forever, David felt totally at peace with his world.

The following week, preparations were well under way for the town's Oktoberfest celebration, although that meant Erin hadn't seen as much of David as she would have liked.

She'd had dinner with him, as well as Angela and Rhett, most evenings and last night he'd knocked on her apartment door at nearly midnight. He'd clearly been exhausted but showed up holding a small bouquet of flowers, which had become his calling card.

"Courting," he whispered into her hair as he wrapped her in a tight hug. "I hope I didn't wake you. I know I should have called or texted first, but I had to see you." He kissed her, then stifled a yawn.

"If this is the kind of energy you put into a booty call," she said with a laugh, leading him into the apartment, "you need to work on your skills."

He nuzzled his face into the crook of her neck. "I have mad skills."

"Trust me, I know." She set the flowers on the counter and turned in his arms. "But you also have dark circles under your eyes."

"Are you offering me makeup?"

"I'm offering," she said, tugging him toward the bedroom, "a few hours of decent sleep. In a real bed, not the couch."

He let out a soft moan. "I hate to admit how good that sounds. I came here with every intention of having my wicked way with you."

"Save your energy for Oktoberfest."

"Only if you promise to wear a dirndl to the competition."

"To match your lederhosen?" she asked, pushing him down onto the bed.

"You know you love my lederhosen," he said sleepily, bending forward to take off his boots.

Erin's heart swelled as she watched him undress. There were so many things about this man that she loved. The way he tried so hard at everything he did—from the brewery to taking care of Rhett to repairing his relationship with his mother. The way he made Erin feel both cherished and challenged—as if he had no doubt she could handle everything life threw at her.

She would have never guessed that the crush she'd had on him for months could so quickly turn into a much deeper connection. But somehow they fit together perfectly. She softened some of his rough edges and he'd helped her unlock her confidence. His belief in her helped her realize she needed to believe in herself.

She'd even gone to see Mari Clayton from the Aspen Foundation, asking the woman to reconsider funding Erin's after-school program. Before David, Erin would have simply accepted the foundation's declining her request. But the program with the kids was too important to give up and she had no doubt any longer that she was the one meant to lead it.

Sugar rose from her place on the pillow next to Erin's

and slowly walked over to rub against David's back. He'd even won over Erin's cantankerous cat.

The past month hadn't been easy, and they were both being pulled in a hundred different directions. But the time they spent together was precious, and Erin wanted to believe they had the basis for something strong and lasting.

She was already in her pajamas, so had no issue crawling into bed next to him when he held up the sheet and comforter. He pulled her in close so her back was against his chest, then draped an arm around her.

"I really did mean to ravish you," he said, dropping a featherlight kiss at the base of her neck.

"Sleep," she whispered, and within seconds felt him relax and heard his breathing slow.

She snuggled in tighter and closed her eyes, happy to fall asleep in David's arms and even happier when she awoke an hour later to find him unbuttoning her pajama top.

"I got my second wind," he told her, and proceeded to make good on all his promises about ravishing and wicked ways.

They made love deep into the night, but he left at dawn, wanting to be back at his place before Rhett woke up.

"Jenna will be out of rehab soon," he told her as he put on his jeans and boots. "She's doing well and can't wait to get back to her son."

"Do you think she's going to be able to stay healthy this time?"

A shadow passed over his face. "She loves Rhett more than anything." He sighed. "I definitely hope she loves him enough to make the alcohol and drugs a thing of the past. My mom is going to stay in town for a while, and I plan to be more involved in Jenna's life, whether she wants it or not."

"You're bringing your family back together." She sat up in the bed, tucking the sheet under her arms. "I'm proud of you."

He stilled as color crept into his cheeks. "Thanks."

"I like making you blush."

"I don't blush," he said, sounding offended, which made her smile.

"You're definitely blushing," she told him with a wink.

Pulling his sweater over his head, he moved toward her, then tugged on the sheet.

Erin yelped and held it tight to her body, but let it slip when he kissed her deeply. "First you hint that I need a nap and now you accuse me of blushing. What's next?"

"Next is you go home before *I* have *my* wicked way with you," she said, squealing when he tickled her.

"So tempting," he whispered. "When my life gets back to normal, I'm taking you away for the weekend. You and me and a hotel room all weekend long."

"I think I'd like that."

"I think you'd love that."

She had to bite her tongue to keep from whispering, *I think I love you.*

But he must have read something in her eyes, because he pulled back suddenly, like she'd scalded him. Definitely too soon for *I love you*, but he was planning weekend trips, which meant something.

He brushed her hair away from her face. "Thank you for tonight."

"Literally my pleasure."

He flashed a lopsided grin, then walked out of her bedroom. She waited until she heard the apartment door close then threw on her robe and went to lock the door. She parted the front curtains and watched him drive away, wondering if she'd ever get used to the thought of David McCay belonging to her.

Chapter Fifteen

"Stop messing with your hair," Melody told Erin Friday night as the two women walked toward the park at the center of downtown Crimson. "You look beautiful."

Erin immediately pressed her hand to her side. "I wasn't messing with my hair. I'm just not used to wearing it down and styled."

"It looks pretty," Melody's daughter, Elaina, told her. "Like you're a princess."

Erin felt a bit like a princess tonight, the first evening of Crimson's Oktoberfest celebration. Melody had convinced her to have her hair done at a local salon and buy a new outfit for the event. Although it was out of her comfort zone, Erin had chosen a chic but casual fitted sweaterdress from the small boutique they'd gone to in Aspen. It had been over her budget but too perfect to pass up. Paired with her vintage cowboy boots and some chunky jewelry she'd borrowed from Melody, she felt amazing and couldn't wait to see David's reaction.

"Thank you, sweetie," Erin said, and smoothed a hand down the girl's blond braid. She nudged Melody, who was pushing her son, Lane, in the stroller. "Do I look like the kind of woman who could attract the town's hottie brewmaster?" she whispered.

"I don't think you need to worry about that," Melody answered with a laugh. "You've already caught him—hook, line and sinker."

"That's right." Erin took a deep breath and whispered, "David McCay is mine." A tiny bubble of happiness floated up inside her. She'd done it. In the space of a month, she'd turned her ordinary life into something extraordinary. It wasn't just David. Karen Henderson, the elementary school's principal, had called Erin into her office the previous afternoon. Apparently she'd fielded calls from several families requesting to be put on a Kidzone waiting list.

While Karen admitted she'd been skeptical at the beginning, Erin's program was turning out to be a valuable asset to the community and great PR for the school district. Mari at the Aspen Foundation had agreed to do another site visit and allowed Erin to resubmit her grant proposal along with letters of recommendation from eight of the ten families who had kids enrolled in the program.

"Where's Daddy?" Elaina asked, gripping Melody's leg. "There are lots of people here."

"He's keeping everyone safe," Melody said gently. "We'll see him when he gets off duty in a little while."

Erin looked around the streets of Crimson, with the shops still brightly lit to take advantage of the Oktoberfest crowds. She hadn't seen so many people converge on downtown since last year's Christmas festival. "It's huge," she said, clapping her hands. "I knew it would be, but I'm so happy for David. He worked hard to make this event a success."

"Apparently lots of people like beer and German food." Melody smiled. "When are the beer contest winners announced?"

Erin glanced at her watch. "In about ten minutes. Let's head to the grandstand. I want to be there when his name is called."

"The supportive girlfriend," Melody said, gently elbowing Erin in the ribs. "It's a good look on you."

Suddenly there was a commotion on the sidewalk in front of them. Melody gripped the stroller as Erin grabbed Elaina's hand, pulling the girl toward the side of the brick building.

A moment later, Joel Martin stood directly in front of her, and she gasped as she saw the flash of a blade in his hand.

"You did this to me," he said, his voice an angry snarl.

Erin's throat went dry even as her heart pounded in her chest. "I don't know what you're talking about," she whispered as she pushed Elaina behind her. "Please put away the knife."

"The hell you don't," he said, his eyes narrowing. "My old lady kicked me out because of you. My kid don't want to talk to me. Your boyfriend made sure I lost my job at the tire store, and now I got nothin'."

She could see a crowd beginning to form in a wide circle around them, and met Melody's gaze behind Joel's shoulder. "Elaina," she whispered. "Go to your Mommy, okay?" She started to give the girl a gentle push but Joel stepped forward.

"Don't move," he shouted. "You don't get to tell no one what to do tonight. Not until I'm done with you."

The little girl buried her face against Erin's leg with a whimper, and Erin saw Melody's face turn white as ash.

"I can't talk to you when you're waving a knife at me," she said, willing her voice to be calm. "Please let the girl go to her mom. She has nothing to do with this."

"You and your damn kids," he muttered. "You think you're so great, like you rule the school."

She shook her head. "I don't think—"

"All this started with that stupid McCay boy. His mama was a hot little piece, but I didn't want nothin' to do with the kid. Now I've got the sheriff breathing down my neck every time I turn around, and my life is in the toilet."

"I'm sorry," she said automatically. Was there anything she could say to this man that would stop his tirade?

"I'm going to make your boyfriend sorry for messing with my life. You'll all be sorry if you don't help me fix it."

Erin swallowed. She hadn't realized David had been in contact with Joel since that day at the community center. What had he done to make this man so angry?

"What can I do?"

She could see more people beginning to gather around them. One man called for Joel to set down the knife, but Joel only brandished it more erratically. Where was Cole Bennett or Melody's husband, Grant, when she needed him?

"You gotta talk to Danielle. Get her to take me back. Tell her I'm a good daddy and I got a right to see my son."

"I don't think—"

"Tell her," he shouted, taking a menacing step forward. At the same time, the crowd parted and Grant Cross muscled his way into their small circle.

"Drop the knife," he commanded, his gaze white-hot.

"Back off," Joel answered, slashing at the air with the weapon.

Elaina let out another little cry and whispered, "Daddy."

Before Erin could stop her, the girl tore away from Erin's embrace and ran toward her father. Grant's attention switched from Joel to his daughter as he moved forward.

Joel thrust out the knife again, just as Elaina ran past. The girl screamed as the blade sliced into her side. Then she crumpled to the ground.

Erin heard another scream that she recognized as Melody's.

Joel was momentarily still, clearly shocked by what he'd done. In those few seconds, Grant made his move, grabbing Joel's wrist and twisting it away from his body. Although Joel struggled, the knife clattered to the ground, and Erin kicked it out of reach. Cole came through the crowd and slapped cuffs on Joel, reading him his rights as Grant bent to his daughter, calling for an ambulance.

Erin rushed toward Melody, who had pulled Lane out of the stroller and was elbowing her way through the crowd to get to Grant and Elaina.

The next few minutes were a blur. Erin took the boy from Melody, who maintained more composure than Erin could have ever imagined. Joel was taken away by another deputy, and Cole turned his attention to crowd control, instructing onlookers to give the Cross family space. Two EMTs were on the scene soon after, and Elaina was placed on a stretcher, then into an ambulance.

Erin handed Lane to a tearful Melody and promised to call Melody's parents and come to the hospital.

As the ambulance disappeared around the corner, Erin felt her knees start to buckle. A strong hand wrapped around her shoulders, and Cole led her to a bench outside one of the nearby shops.

"Is Elaina going to be okay?" she asked, fighting back tears. The EMTs had loaded the girl into the ambulance, but she'd looked so pale against the bright streak of blood staining the front of her unicorn T-shirt.

"The blade penetrated high," Cole said, rubbing a hand over his face. "We've got to hope it didn't hit a lung or major artery."

Nausea washed through Erin, forcing her to bend forward and swallow hard to keep from throwing up all over Cole's shiny black work boots.

"I should have never let her dash away from me," she whispered.

"Don't blame yourself." Cole reached out a hand and squeezed her shoulder. "Joel Martin might be pissed about his life, but he had no business with that knife."

"He reeked of liquor."

"Probably high on something, too." Cole sighed. "I know you want to get to the hospital, but I need to ask you a few questions first."

"Of course. Let me call Melody's parents, then I'll talk to you."

Cole nodded. "I've got to do some crowd control and make an announcement to keep everyone down here calm." He looked out toward the center of the park. "I can already see the news moving through the crowd. Are you going to be okay?"

Erin wanted to scream that she wouldn't be okay until she knew Elaina would recover, but nodded instead.

Cole studied her a moment longer. "My squad car is parked at the curb. If you want to avoid talking to people, I can put you in there for some privacy."

"I'm fine. Go on, Cole." As he walked away, she managed to get her phone out of her purse. Unfortunately, her hands were shaking so badly she couldn't hold them steady enough to access Melody's parents' number in her contacts. Tears spilled onto the phone's screen, and she tried to blink them back. Now was not the time to lose it.

She finally made the call, her heart breaking as Melody's mother began to sob loudly on the other end of the line. She spoke to Melody's father, who remained calmer and promised to get his wife to the hospital.

She'd just returned her phone to her purse when David raced up to her and hauled her into his arms. "Did that scumbag hurt you?" he asked, breathless as he held her tight against him. "I'll kill him if he hurt you."

She wanted so much to sink into him and take the comfort that he offered. Instead, she pulled back. "Did you get Joel fired from his job?"

"What?" David seemed confused by the question.

"Joel said we'd ruined his life and that you made him lose his job."

His gaze turned steely. "Yeah, I talked to the guy who owns the tire store—told him he needs to pay attention to the sort of people he hired."

She moved away, out of the warmth and safety of his embrace. "Why would you do that?"

"You're kidding, right? I did it because the guy screwed with my sister, then his son bullied my nephew." He held out his hands. "Clearly tonight is evidence that Joel is a loose cannon. I figured he'd move on if he didn't have a job. You'd already told me his girlfriend had kicked him to the curb. I didn't like the idea of him being anywhere near Rhett or you during the after-school program or still in town when Jenna returns."

It felt like her heart had taken a direct hit. "I shared the information about Danielle Rodriguez in confidence. If you had concerns about Rhett's safety while under my care, you should have come to me about it."

"What would you have done?"

"Assured you that I had things under control," she answered, trying to ignore the fact that he hadn't denied having doubts about her ability to keep his nephew safe.

"Like things were under control tonight and a little girl ended up in the hospital?"

"That wasn't my fault," she insisted, even though she'd said almost the same thing to Cole minutes earlier.

His blue eyes turned hard. "Are you saying it's mine?"

"I'm saying that by trying to control everything without talking to me, you put me at risk."

"I was trying to protect you," he said, his voice tight.

There had been a time when Erin believed she needed a man to take care of things for her, and she still wanted someone to rely on in her life. But not like this. She'd just come to realize her self-worth and wasn't about to let anyone, even David, diminish it now.

"I don't need you to protect me," she whispered. "I need—"

"Join the club," he muttered, walking away several steps before stalking back to her. "My sister didn't want my help. My mother thinks she can handle everything just fine without me. I thought you were different."

"I thought *you* believed in me," she countered.

"I do."

She shook her head. "Not if you're going behind my back to handle things that involve me. That isn't trust."

"It's how I take care of the people I love."

Silence stretched between them, fraught with tension.

Was she included in the people he loved? Was he actually trying to say the words she longed to hear? She shook off her curiosity because the whole thing was twisted now.

"You didn't think I could handle it." Her voice shook as she said the words, but she tipped up her chin, refusing to ignore the crux of the problem.

"You're a kindergarten teacher," he said, as if that explained everything.

She felt her eyes widen and he quickly added, "You have no experience dealing with people like Joel Martin."

"Really?" She stepped forward and jabbed her finger into his chest. "You think I don't see bullies working at an elementary school?"

"He's more than a bully, and we both know it."

"And apparently because I'm *just* a kindergarten teacher, you don't have to share things with me."

"I never said *just*."

"I know what you meant." She shook her head. "I've got to give a statement to Cole so I can get to the hospital."

"I'll drive you."

"No. Tonight is important to you."

"Not as important as you."

She studied him for a moment, willing those words to be true. But everything he'd said to her earlier seemed to refute that. Even the way he'd used the word *love* seemed wrong.

"I thought you were different," she whispered. "I thought you believed I could handle anything. That I was strong and capable." She gave a quiet laugh. "You made *me* believe in myself. And now..."

"Now what?" He moved closer, but she didn't back away.

"Now I can't go back to who I was before. I want more, David. I deserve more."

"I thought I could give you that."

She lifted her hand and trailed her fingers over the rough stubble that shadowed his jaw. "I did, too. We were both wrong."

Then she turned and hurried to where Cole Bennett waited next to his patrol car.

"Everything okay?" the sheriff asked, one brow raised as he watched the place she knew David stood behind her.

"No," she answered honestly. "But it will be. I'm ready to answer your questions."

"You won!" Tracie raced from behind the bar and threw her arms around David when he finally made it back to Elevation after Oktoberfest ended for the evening.

There was a loud round of applause from the bar's patrons, many of whom had come to Elevation to celebrate after the event.

He gave them a half-hearted wave and tried to muster a smile, but his insides were churning with a mix of guilt and regret. He'd beat out two dozen other breweries to win top honors at the festival and a nationally known distribution company had approached him about bottling not only his Altitude IPA, the award-winning beer, but two of his other more popular selections.

He couldn't care less.

"What's wrong?" Tracie asked when she took in his expression. "Did you hear an update on the Cross girl?"

"As far as I know, she's still in surgery." Bile rose in David's throat as he spoke the words. The knife blade had nicked Elaina's right lung, and she'd been rushed into the OR as soon as she arrived at the hospital. Cole Bennett had driven Erin to the hospital, then come back downtown to oversee the end of Oktoberfest, but David knew the sheriff would be back with the family and the Crosses' friends now, waiting for word on the little girl.

"She's going to be okay," Tracie whispered, with more confidence than David felt.

"It was my fault." He rubbed a hand over his face. "If I hadn't antagonized him..."

"You didn't put the knife in his hand or tell him to come after Erin."

"I knew he was unstable and a drug user. I wanted to mess with his life, to make him angry for his role in Jenna's relapse and how he'd treated Erin. I should have let it go."

"You couldn't have known how he'd go off."

"No," David agreed, "but it doesn't change that he did."

He'd told Erin he wanted to protect her, and that was true, but it had been anger fueling him when he'd interfered with Joel Martin's life. Now an innocent girl was paying the price for David's mistake.

Elaina was the same age as Rhett. His nephew had talked about the girl several times, and David couldn't imagine what that family was going through right now because of him.

"David."

"I'm fine, Tracie," he said when the bartender continued to study him. "Don't worry about me. Get back to work. I need to go upstairs and check on Rhett."

She watched him a few more moments. "I'm still happy for your success tonight," she said, squeezing his arm as she moved past him. "You've worked hard for it."

One of his regular customers walked by and patted him on the back. "Nice work tonight, McCay. Why don't you come to the back room and have a celebratory drink with us? One of the ladies is asking about you."

"Thanks, Brad." David forced a smile. "I'll be over in a minute."

This had been his life before Rhett and Erin, and up until a few weeks ago, he'd been happy with it. Or at least he hadn't realized what he was missing. He'd been given a taste of how much better his life could be, but somehow he'd managed to muck up the whole thing before he'd even had a chance to truly claim it.

Maybe this was all he was meant to be. The local brewery owner who'd share a couple drinks with patrons or a few hours with a willing woman before retreating to his solitary existence.

No harm, no foul. Nobody got hurt.

Which didn't explain the searing pain that burned across his chest, refusing to ease.

Brad turned and gestured to him, hitching his thumb at the cute blonde standing at his right side. The woman offered David a slow, sexy smile full of promise. The exact kind of promise he needed to numb his brain and his body and forget about the things he couldn't control and what he'd lost because of it.

David slipped into his apartment later that night—or in the early morning hours of the following day, to be exact. He'd stayed at Elevation until closing but had refused the lovely blonde's offer of a nightcap in her hotel room.

His life might be in the toilet, but he was no longer the man he used to be—the one who would flush it away with no thought of the consequences.

Cole had texted to say Elaina was still in surgery, so David grabbed a pillow and blanket from the side table and started to make up his temporary bed on the couch.

Once Jenna returned, he'd have his apartment to himself again. He had visions of Erin spending the night here in his big bed and the thought of waking up after a full night's sleep wrapped around her body still made his heart clench. After tonight, he wasn't sure his fantasies would ever become a reality.

"Uncle David?"

Rhett stood in the doorway to the hall, sleepily rubbing his eyes.

"Hey, buddy, why aren't you asleep?"

"Is Elaina going to be okay?"

"The doctors are doing everything they can for her," he answered, moving toward the boy. He crouched down until they were at eye level. "I know she's a friend of yours."

Rhett nodded. "She was my girlfriend but then she started dating Micah from the other class. We're still friends, though. Her favorite color is purple."

"Then let's go out tomorrow and buy her a get-well gift that's purple." He lifted the boy into his arms and walked toward the bedroom. "Do you have a different girlfriend?"

"No, I still like Elaina. She got mad when Isaac and I got in a fight."

"You're definitely my nephew," David muttered. "Sorry to tell you this, but you're in for a lifetime of girl troubles if you take after me. So don't, okay?"

"Is Ms. MacDonald your girlfriend?" Rhett asked as David lowered him to the bed.

"I don't know," David answered honestly. "I think I messed it up."

"By fighting?"

"Sort of," David admitted.

He pulled the sheet around the boy and leaned in to drop a kiss on Rhett's forehead.

"Will you stay with me until I fall asleep?"

The nightlight plugged into an outlet on the far wall cast a soft glow across the room. Rhett looked so small and innocent tucked into bed, and it killed David how much the boy had seen and experienced during his young life. Childhood was supposed to be about building forts and sneaking an extra cookie after dinner, not having a mother taken to rehab and a friend stabbed on a busy street.

When bad things had happened to David as a kid, he'd had Jenna to lean on. He couldn't even count the number of nights he'd dragged his pillow and blanket into her tiny room and slept on the floor next to her bed so neither of them had to be alone.

But even though he might not be the world's best role model, David was the person Rhett had as his own.

He toed off his boots, then drew back the covers. "Scoot over," he told the boy, and got into the bed. His feet hung over the edge and Rhett had left him only a small corner of the pillow, but when the boy reached out in the dark and wrapped his small hand around David's larger one, there was no place in the world David would have rather been.

He closed his eyes and tried to control the emotions pummeling him from every angle. In the dark, listening to Rhett's steady breathing, it was difficult to tamp down the regret and pain coursing through him at the knowledge that he'd very likely lost Erin.

Maybe he could find some stupid late-night movie on TV and try to forget—or at least ignore—the mess he'd made. His plan was to leave as soon as Rhett fell back to sleep, but the next time he opened his eyes, light streamed through the curtains.

"You snore," Rhett told him matter-of-factly.

David blinked at the boy, whose face was directly in front of his on the pillow. "I don't snore," he said, his voice rough. How had he managed to sleep the whole night in this tiny bed? "And you kicked me."

Rhett grinned. "I know. Mommy says I sleep like a starfish."

"You remember she's coming back in a week, right?"

"She said we can move into our new house."

"Yep." David pulled in a deep breath. He'd finally convinced Jenna to let him help her with rent on a cozy duplex on the south end of town. The three-bedroom house had a small fenced yard in the back and was in a neighborhood of young families, stable professionals and a few older couples who had been there for decades.

Angela was going to stay with them until Jenna was ready to handle life on her own again. They had a lot of work to do to keep his sister on the right path, and David hoped a decent rental house was a good first step. At least it was something he could control, unlike everything else in his life.

"There's a yard and a park at the end of the block," he told Rhett. "The last time I drove by I saw kids playing soccer on one of the fields."

Rhett scrunched up his nose. "I'm not good at soccer."

"Says who?"

The boy shrugged. "I never played."

"Well, you can learn." David sat up and stretched his legs. His back ached and there was a kink in his neck, but it was worth it because Rhett seemed happy. "We'll buy a ball today."

"You play baseball."

"I can play soccer, too." He moved to the edge of the bed. "At least I played when I was your age. I must remember something."

Rhett looked unconvinced. "That was a long time ago."

"Thanks for the reminder." David grabbed his phone from where he'd left it on the dresser. Several texts had come through overnight, but the one that made his heart lighten was from Cole. He turned back to Rhett. "Elaina made it through surgery and is resting now."

"She's okay?"

"She's going to be fine."

"We can get her a purple soccer ball," Rhett announced

as he placed Ruffie on top of the pillow. "Me and her can both learn to play."

"She and I," David said automatically, then swallowed. He was correcting the boy's grammar like a parent would do.

"I thought I heard voices," his mother said from the doorway.

Rhett pointed at David. "We had a sleepover."

A smile tugged at the corner of Angela's mouth. "Your Uncle David snores."

Rhett laughed. "I told you so," he said to David.

David bent and gathered the boy in his arms, lifting him high in the air then pretending to let go before catching him again. "I'll teach you to make fun of me."

Rhett squirmed and giggled and finally shouted, "I got to pee."

David immediately set him on the ground. "Well played, buddy."

"Go to the bathroom and get dressed," Angela told the boy. "I'm going to take you and your uncle out to breakfast."

"Pancakes," Rhett yelled, then grabbed a wad of clothes from the floor and ran toward the bathroom.

"Clean clothes," Angela called after him.

David smiled. "I don't think I cared about clean clothes until—"

"You cared about girls," his mother supplied.

"True enough." He massaged a hand along the back of his neck and turned to make Rhett's bed. "I can't believe I slept the night in here."

"You'll be glad to get us out of your hair when Jenna comes back."

"It hasn't been so bad," he said, surprised to find he

meant the words. "But living above the bar isn't the best for a five-year-old boy."

"You've taken good care of him," his mother said gently.

David's chest pinched as he thought of the price an innocent girl had paid for him trying to protect his nephew.

He turned to find that his mother had stepped farther into the room. "Last night wasn't your fault."

"She's going to be okay," David said, not addressing her comment directly. "She made it out of surgery."

Angela nodded. "Still doesn't make it your fault."

"I wanted to hurt Joel Martin." He swallowed to stave off the anger that rose in his throat at the thought of the man. "I purposely messed with his life to get back at him for giving Jenna the drugs."

"She took them," Angela said. "Your sister has to work out her demons on her own, David."

"Demons that are there because I didn't protect her," he countered, then added softly, "Because I didn't protect either of you."

Tears shone in his mother's pale blue eyes, still so striking after all these years. "How do you think I feel? I was the one who trusted that creep around my daughter. I let him into my home and—"

"You didn't know."

"I should have." She gave a humorless laugh. "Jenna knew. She hated him from the start."

"You did the best you could at the time."

"How is it you can forgive me but not yourself?"

Her voice was like a caress, the gentle motherly tone he'd always wanted to hear when he'd been a kid. The way he heard Jenna talk to Rhett. For all of his sister's problems, she loved her son. David hoped for all their sakes it would be enough to help her vanquish her issues once and for all.

But he couldn't release the belief that he'd failed his sister and his mother. Just like he'd failed Erin last night. No matter what his intention had been, the outcome was what mattered.

"I'm going to take a quick shower," he told his mother without answering her question.

He started to walk past her, but she threw her arms around his waist and hugged him tight. "You're a good man, David. I love you."

Emotion rushed through him like a tidal wave, turning him into the vulnerable boy he'd been so many years ago. He couldn't remember ever hearing his mother say she loved him, and so he'd convinced himself he didn't need the words.

One more delusion shattered.

He hugged her back and whispered, "I love you, too," then broke free of the embrace and left the room. If he allowed himself to feel anything, there was a good chance he'd have to feel everything.

And an even better chance he'd never recover.

Chapter Sixteen

A week after the accident, Erin parked her car outside the Crosses' two-story house in a newer subdivision west of Crimson. She opened the back of her car and pulled out gifts from the staff and students at Crimson Elementary that she'd offered to bring to the family.

Elaina had been released from the hospital the previous afternoon but still had a few more days of rest at home before she could return to school.

Erin had canceled Kidzone for the week, and quite possibly for good. She couldn't bear the idea that Elaina had been injured because Erin had angered a parent and he'd come looking for revenge.

What if she couldn't keep them safe? There were district-sponsored security measures in place at school, but the responsibility for her students during the after-school program was completely hers.

She wanted to believe she could handle anything, but

Friday night's tragedy had rocked her confidence to its core. Her mother had always told her to be satisfied with good enough, but Erin hadn't listened. She'd wanted more from life—to be more.

But not at the cost of a child's life.

She had two big boxes filled with stuffed animals and games plus several trays of meals to deliver. Instead of making two trips, she piled everything into her arms, trying to distribute the weight as best she could. A few steps up the front walk she realized her mistake. One of the boxes began to teeter, and she tried to adjust her hold so everything would fall back into balance.

Instead, the lasagna she'd placed on top of her load started to slide and would have splattered to the ground if a set of strong hands hadn't stopped it.

"Whoa, there," David said against her ear, his arms coming around her to steady the pile. "You may have bitten off more than you can chew with this one, darlin'."

Erin gritted her teeth. Didn't that just about sum up her life at the moment?

"I've got it under control," she said, even though it was obvious she didn't have anything under control.

"I know you do," he agreed, "but can I help anyway?"

She wanted to turn down his offer, to prove that she could handle this one tiny task. But a homemade lasagna would inevitably end up all over the concrete.

"Thanks," she muttered as he took three boxes off her pile.

"We got Elaina a purple soccer ball," Rhett said as he skipped up the walkway next to her. "'Cause Uncle David is going to teach her like he teached me."

"He taught you," Erin corrected with a smile. "I saw you playing at recess today."

"I made a goal." He held up an oversize gift bag. "I

bringed her a pink baseball bat, too, so we can learn to play baseball."

"Brought," both Erin and David said at the same time. One small word, yet Erin felt the connection between them zing to life and did her best to ignore it.

David had made his choice by not believing in her, and she'd made hers as a result. There was no going back now.

She knocked to announce their arrival, then they walked into the house together. Lane toddled down the hall toward them, followed by Grant.

"Whett, Whett, Whett," the boy called.

"I don't know who's more excited for your visit," Grant told Rhett. "Elaina or her brother." He glanced at Erin. "Thanks for bringing all of Elaina's stuff. Did you guys come together?"

"No." Erin and David answered simultaneously once more, and Erin felt a blush creep up her cheeks.

Grant looked between them with raised eyebrows. "Okay, then. Elaina's on the couch in the family room," he said to Rhett. "Lane can lead you back there."

"Come on," Lane shouted at the top of his lungs, because he seemed to have no volume control. Rhett followed the boy, leaving Erin standing with David and Grant in the small foyer.

"I'm going to put everything in the kitchen," she said, feeling suddenly self-conscious. She'd spent a lot of time at the hospital with Melody but hadn't talked to Grant since the night Elaina was hurt. Not since he'd watched Erin let his daughter run past the man holding a knife.

One glance at David showed he looked as uncomfortable as she felt. Instead of taking solace in that, Erin wanted to reach out and comfort him.

"I have something to say to both of you." Grant moved to block her way down the narrow hall.

"You don't need to do this." David shifted slightly to stand between her and Grant, as if shielding her from whatever the stoic deputy might tell them.

"I don't blame either of you for Elaina's injury," he said, ignoring David. "And it's obvious you each blame yourself or each other. I can't tell which it is, but I want you to stop."

"I should never have let go of her," Erin blurted, fresh tears clogging her throat. She'd already cried so much since Friday night but her heart was a bottomless reservoir of guilt.

"No one would have been in that situation if I hadn't antagonized Martin," David said, more to her than Grant. "If anyone is at fault—"

"Someone is at fault." Grant's voice was firm. "Joel Martin. We're going to make sure he pays for what he did to my little girl. But the blame is solely his, and I want you both to understand that. I've had the worst couple of days of my life and I'm not going to stand here and argue. Do I make myself clear?"

Grant might not be in uniform at the moment, but he still commanded respect. Erin knew it was pointless to argue with him.

"Thank you," she whispered. Trying to discreetly wipe her eyes on her sleeve, she moved past him to the kitchen.

As she placed the packages on the counter, she felt David at her side.

"Listen to Grant," he said, setting the boxes he carried next to hers.

"I could tell you the same thing."

"But you won't," he countered, "because we both know I set off that guy. I only wanted to—"

"Don't say 'protect me.'" Fists clenched at her sides, Erin turned to him. "I can't do this with you again, David."

His lips pressed together in a firm line, but he nodded. "When are you going to reopen the program?"

The question caught her off guard.

"Rhett keeps asking," he added. "I guess he's been working on something for Jenna when she comes back."

Erin smiled even as a band of emotion tightened around her chest. "It's an adventure book—pictures of all the things he wants them to do together. He's been putting a lot of time into it."

"He's worried about finishing before she returns."

There were so many things unfinished right now. Erin hated letting go of Kidzone, but panic pounded through her every time she thought of Joel Martin and what could have happened if he'd chosen to confront her during her program hours at the community center. "I'll bring it to school, and he can work on it there."

"You didn't answer the question," he said softly.

"I'm a kindergarten teacher." She cleared her throat when her voice cracked. "You said it yourself. I'm not a social worker or someone trained to work with families in crisis. I had an idea for a way to help but…"

"It was a great idea." He leaned in so they were at eye level. "It still is."

"Maybe Olivia can find a person better qualified—"

"Kidzone belongs to you."

Her heart squeezed at the tenderness in his tone. She'd wanted the program to be hers, just like she'd wanted to believe David belonged to her. But in the last few days she'd never felt more alone.

"I've got to go," she whispered, turning from him. It was too hard to pretend she was fine when her heart wouldn't stop breaking. "Tell Melody I'll talk to her later."

"Erin," he called as she hurried away, but she didn't

stop. Couldn't stop. Not when she might crumble into a million sad pieces if she did.

"You turn your foot just a little," Rhett shouted, "then look up and kick!"

Elaina Cross clapped as Rhett shot the soccer ball toward the goal David had set up on the far end of the backyard. She sat bundled up on a patio chair watching Rhett teach Lane how to kick the ball. Both boys ran across the yard, Rhett slowing his pace to match the toddler's. David's stomach tightened when Lane stumbled, but Rhett took the boy's hand and they continued together.

"He's sweet with Lane," Melody said gently.

"Yeah," David agreed, pride creeping into his tone. "He's a good kid. Thanks for letting him visit Elaina."

"She's thrilled. Now that she feels better it's difficult to rest all day."

"She looks good." David glanced at Melody. "She'll make a hundred percent recovery, right?"

"According to the doctor," Melody answered.

David nodded. "I have to tell you how sorry—"

"Grant spoke to you," Melody interrupted.

"He did."

"Then no apologies. There's only one person responsible for Elaina's injury, and it isn't you."

"Or Erin," David added automatically.

"Of course not," Melody agreed with a sigh. "Although I can't get her to believe that."

"You have to convince her to reopen the Kidzone program."

"What are you talking about?" Melody turned fully to face him, shock and concern warring in her tone.

"She isn't running the program. You didn't know?"

Melody shook her head. "I've been kind of preoccupied."

"I thought it was temporary, but the way she sounded today…"

"We can't let her do that."

Lane shouted for his mommy to watch him kick, and Melody called out a few words of encouragement. When the boys were occupied again, her gaze swung back to David. "Crimson needs that program. *Erin* needs that program."

David rubbed a hand against the back of his neck. "I said some things Friday night," he admitted.

"I'm guessing they were stupid things?" Melody crossed her arms over her chest.

"Really stupid," he agreed.

"Fix it," she told him.

"I can't. Erin ended—"

"Do you love her?"

"I don't… I mean…she deserves more than—"

"Simple question. Do you love her?"

David felt himself shift uncomfortably under Melody's steely gaze. The woman barely reached his chest, but she was a force to be reckoned with nonetheless.

"I love her," he whispered.

"Then fix it," she repeated.

He opened his mouth to argue, then shut it again. He was used to working hard but had never had to put himself on the line emotionally. Hard work and commitment, he was quickly discovering, were two different things.

Yes, he loved Erin. She was the best thing that had ever happened to him, like winning the relationship lottery—unexpected and wholly life-changing. But what if he tried to make things right and she still said no?

What if he wasn't enough?

He started to shake his head, but Rhett looked over at that moment, flashing a wide grin as he dribbled the ball toward Elaina. Joy radiated from the boy with such intensity it stole David's breath. A month ago he would have never guessed Rhett could look that happy. David might not have known what he was doing when he stepped in to care for his nephew, but that hadn't stopped him from trying.

And he sure as hell had no idea how to be a man worthy of Erin's love, but he knew for certain he couldn't win her back if he didn't try.

He glanced down at Melody, already feeling a strange sense of accomplishment, and grinned when she gave him an approving nod.

"I have an idea," he told her. "But I'm going to need a lot of help to pull it off."

"You've got it," she answered immediately. "Anything for Erin."

David took a deep breath, resolve filling him. *Anything* to win back Erin.

"Any place but Elevation." Erin refused to budge from where she stood on the sidewalk as Melody and Suzie tried to tug her forward.

"I'm craving artichoke dip," Melody insisted. "You can't deny me after what I've been through."

"Seriously?" Erin glared at her best friend. "You're using Elaina's injury as a ploy to force me to see David? That's shameless."

It was Friday night, exactly two weeks after the confrontation with Joel Martin, and her girlfriends had wrangled Erin into agreeing to a happy hour downtown. The truth was she needed a night out and away from her lonely apartment.

Even the promise of a BBC movie marathon had done little to lift her spirits. All she could think of was the nights she'd spent with David and how much comfier her bed was with his arms wrapped around her.

She hadn't seen him since the afternoon at Melody's house, although Rhett and a few of the other kids continued to ask when Kidzone was going to open again. Even Erin's principal had gently suggested she continue the program, but Erin couldn't bring herself to take that chance again.

How could she expect parents to trust their kids with her when she didn't trust herself?

"I'm not forcing you to talk to him," Melody argued.

"Even though," Suzie added, "you're clearly miserable without him."

"I'm not miserable." Erin bit down on the inside of her cheek to keep from saying more. She was *beyond* miserable, brokenhearted in a way she hadn't known existed. How had she ever believed falling in love was worth this kind of pain?

"Artichoke dip will make you feel better," Melody said, wrapping an arm around Erin's waist.

Erin gave a small laugh. There was no sense arguing, and she couldn't avoid David forever. Crimson was too small a town for that kind of blessing. "Fine. He might not even be here. His sister is home now. They're probably out as a family."

"Probably," Melody said, her voice uncharacteristically high-pitched.

"What's the matter?" Erin asked. "You sound strange."

"I'm hungry," Melody said. "For—"

"Artichoke dip," Erin said, then stopped outside the brewery's front door. "Are you pregnant again? I've never seen you with such a strong craving."

"Just go in already," Suzie muttered.

"Fine," Erin agreed, throwing open the heavy walnut door and striding through. "Are you both happy now?"

"Yes," Melody whispered over her shoulder. "And I hope you will be, too."

Erin didn't have a chance to ask what her friend meant because a loud chorus of cheers rang out from the crowd filling the bar.

She glanced around and saw people she knew from every facet of her life. Teachers, parents and kids from the elementary school; Karen Henderson, the school's principal; as well as Sara and Josh Travers and their group of friends. There were people she'd gone to high school with and even her mother waved to her from a seat at one of the high-top tables in front of the bar.

"What is this?" She automatically took a step back, but Melody pushed her forward.

"You finally taking center stage," her friend whispered as David came out from behind the bar.

"It's a fund-raiser," he said, moving closer. "For you and Crimson Kidzone."

"But the program isn't—"

"Going to start up again until next week," he said loudly. "That's what I told Ms. Clayton from the foundation."

He gestured over his shoulder to where Mari Clayton from the Aspen Foundation stood at the edge of the crowd. The woman gave Erin the thumbs-up and Erin waved in return before her gaze slammed into David's once more.

"This town needs Kidzone," David continued, taking another step toward her, "and the program needs you, darlin'. Everyone in Crimson agrees." He lifted his hands. "Don't we, everyone?"

There was another round of applause and shouts of support. Erin's heart thudded and she pressed her fingers to her wet cheeks as a hush fell over the room. "I don't know what to say," she whispered.

"Say you won't give up." David reached out and covered her hands with his, wiping away her tears with the pads of his thumbs. "On yourself or on me."

A woman's voice cut through the quiet. "Even though he sometimes acts like an idiot."

"Thanks, Mom," David muttered, lacing his fingers with Erin's.

Erin tried not to laugh as she met Angela's brilliant blue gaze across the bar. The older woman stood next to her daughter, who was holding tight to Rhett's hand and looking somewhat uncomfortable as people turned to stare at their small group.

"Mommy's back," Rhett shouted to Erin.

Erin saw color flood Jenna's cheeks, but the woman stepped forward. "I'm very grateful to you and your program," she said, clearing her throat when her voice cracked. "I'm grateful for the support you gave Rhett while I was getting help. This community needs more people like you."

There was another round of applause, and Erin felt her face grow hot. "Everyone is staring at me," she said quietly.

"Because you're amazing," David said. "This town needs you." He pressed a gentle kiss to her knuckles. "But not as much as I need you."

She sucked in a breath at his words. "David."

"Don't say no yet." He squeezed her fingers. "I know I've said stupid things and done stupid things, but please give me another chance. I love you, Erin. I love who you are—your heart and your beauty. I love that you make me want to try harder than I ever have. You make me believe that I can be the type of man you deserve. Let me prove it to you."

She swallowed against the sob that rose in her throat. "You don't have to prove anything to me, David. I love you just the way you are."

"I'm not perfect," he told her.

"You're perfect for me," she countered.

"I know you want a hero."

She lifted up on tiptoe and kissed the corner of his lips. "I want *you*," she whispered, then laughed as he enveloped her in a hug so tight she knew he'd never let her go.

There were more cheers but Erin barely heard them over the wild beating of her own heart. David kissed her deeply.

"Forever," he said when he finally pulled back to look at her. His blue eyes shone with so much love. The intensity of it made her breath catch.

"Forever," she agreed, knowing this moment was just the start to the grandest adventure she could ever imagine.

* * * * *

Love this book? Look for Caden's story, available December 2017 from Harlequin Special Edition! And catch up with all the residents of Crimson in previous books in the CRIMSON, COLORADO *miniseries:*

CHRISTMAS ON CRIMSON MOUNTAIN
ALWAYS THE BEST MAN
A BABY AND A BETROTHAL
A VERY CRIMSON CHRISTMAS

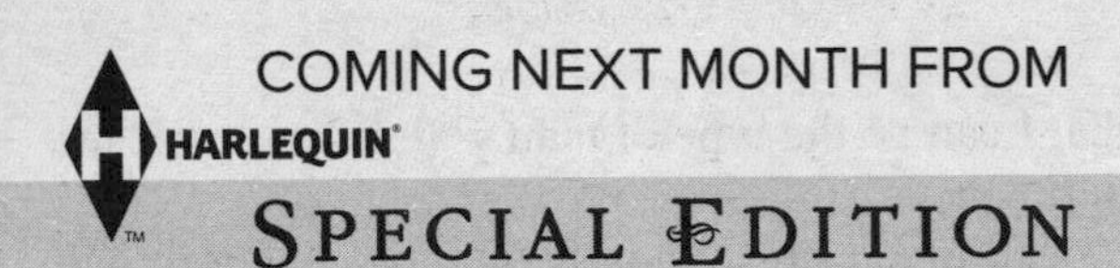

Available September 19, 2017

#2575 GARRET BRAVO'S RUNAWAY BRIDE

The Bravos of Justice Creek • by Christine Rimmer

When Cami Lockwood, wedding gown and all, stumbles onto his campfire after escaping a wedding she never wanted, Garrett Bravo is determined to send the offbeat heiress on her way as soon as he possibly can. But when she decides to stay, he starts to realize his bachelor status is in danger—and he doesn't even mind.

#2576 A CONARD COUNTY COURTSHIP

Conard County: The Next Generation • by Rachel Lee

Vanessa Welling never wanted to return to Conard City, but an unsought inheritance forces her to face unwelcome memories. But Tim Dawson and his son have dealt with grief of their own and when they open their hearts to Vanessa, she's not sure she'll be able to push them away.

#2577 THE MAVERICK'S RETURN

Montana Mavericks: The Great Family Roundup
by Marie Ferrarella

Daniel Stockton fled Rust Creek after the death of his parents ten years ago. Now he's back and trying to mend fences with his siblings—and Anne Lattimore. But he's about to realize he left more than his high school sweetheart behind all those years ago...

#2578 THE COWBOY WHO GOT AWAY

Celebration, TX • by Nancy Robards Thompson

After years of travel and adventure to find themselves, champion bull rider Jude Campbell and accidental wedding planner Juliette Lowell are reunited in their hometown of Celebration. But will their new hopes and dreams once again get in the way of their chance at a life together?

#2579 DO YOU TAKE THIS BABY?

The Men of Thunder Ridge • by Wendy Warren

When Ethan Ladd becomes guardian to his nephew, he's determined to be the best father he can. There's only one catch: to ensure Cody doesn't end up in foster care, Ethan needs a wife. Luckily, local college professor Gemma Gould is head over heels for baby Cody and is willing to take on a marriage of convenience!

#2580 BIDDING ON THE BACHELOR

Saved by the Blog • by Kerri Carpenter

Recently divorced Carissa Blackwell returns to her hometown and reconnects with her first love, Jasper Dumont—can they rekindle an old flame while the ubiquitous Bayside Blogger reports their every move?

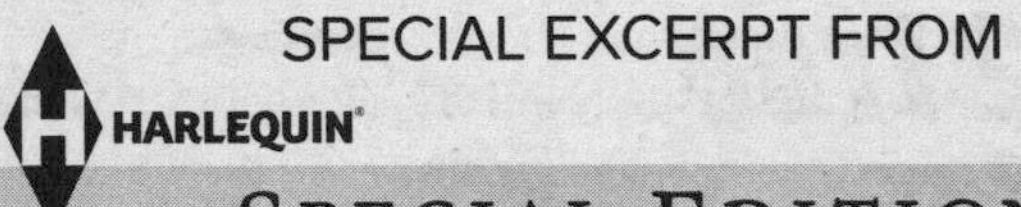

When wedding-gown-clad Cami Lockwood stumbles onto his campfire, Garrett Bravo's first instinct is to send her away—ASAP—but now his bachelor status is in danger and he's surprised to find he doesn't even care.

Read on for a sneak preview of,
GARRETT BRAVO'S RUNAWAY BRIDE,
the next book in New York Times *bestselling author*
Christine Rimmer's
THE BRAVOS OF JUSTICE CREEK *miniseries.*

"Munchy!" Cami cried. The mutt raced to greet her and she dipped low to meet him.

Garrett waited, giving her all the time she wanted to pet and praise his dog. When she finally looked at him again, he explained, "The bear must have whacked him a good one. When I found him, he was knocked out, but I think he's fine now."

She submitted to more doggy kisses. "Oh, you sweet boy. I'm so glad you're all right…"

When she finally stood up again, he handed over the diamond ring and that giant purse.

"Thank you, Garrett," she said very softly, slipping the ring into the pocket of the jeans she'd borrowed from him. "I seem to be saying that a lot lately, but I really do mean it every time."

"Did you want those high-heeled shoes with the red soles? I can go back and get them…" When she just shook her head, he asked, "You sure?" He eyed her bare feet. "Looks like you might need them."

HSEEXP0917

"I still have your flip-flops. They're up by the Jeep. I kicked them off when I ran after Munch." For a long, sweet moment, they just grinned at each other. Then she said kind of breathlessly, "It all could have gone so terribly wrong."

"But it didn't."

She caught her lower lip between her pretty white teeth. "I was so scared."

"Hey." He brushed a hand along her arm, just to reassure her. "You're okay. And Munch is fine."

She drew in a shaky breath and then, well, somehow it just happened. She dropped the purse. When she reached out, so did he.

He pulled her into his arms and breathed in the scent of her skin, so fresh and sweet with a hint of his own soap and shampoo. He heard the wind through the trees, a bird calling far off—and Munch at their feet, happily panting.

It was a fine moment and he savored the hell out of it.

"Garrett," she whispered, like his name was her secret. And she tucked her blond head under his chin. She felt so good, so soft in all the right places. He wrapped her tighter in his arms and almost wished he would never have to let her go.

Which was crazy. He'd just met her last night, hardly knew her at all. And yesterday she'd almost married some other guy.

HSEEXP0917